I0539661

The Man Who Holds the Whip

SHOSHANNA EVERS

Copyright © 2012, 2014 Shoshanna Evers

All rights reserved.

ISBN-10: 0988753723
ISBN-13: 978-0-9887537-2-3

CONTENTS

Table of Contents

DEDICATION

For those who sometimes fall asleep,
dreaming of beautiful man, holding a whip...

CHAPTER ONE

Grace Pontaine didn't bother to change out of her scrubs when she stomped in the door—a top priority, usually. Tonight, a glass of merlot needed to come first, followed by a bath, perhaps, or some long-overdue meditation. Anything to erase her hellish day. In her whole five years of nursing, Grace had never felt so demeaned by a doctor as she had today.

It shouldn't bother her, since he probably had a miserable life anyway, but it did. She knew what she was talking about and being yelled at like a child in front of her patients was just…screw it.

Wine.

The merlot in the bottom of the cabinet had a twist cap and no cork, so she wasn't expecting a fine wine. But it didn't need to taste good, it just needed to work. Grace didn't bother giving the red liquid a chance to breathe—or whatever it was she was supposed to do before taking sip—preferring to drink a full glass while still standing at her kitchen counter, contemplating her options.

Quit work? *I wish.*

Get drunk and forget about it? More likely.

Text Ian.

No. No. No. She always texted him when she was upset or drunk, as if he hadn't broken her heart—smashed it into a million little pieces when he dumped her three years ago. Taking another fortifying gulp of the wine, Grace pulled her phone out of the side pocket of her scrub pants, the cargo-pants style she preferred because it afforded her the ability to carry a ton of stuff on her at work.

At least Ian always texted back. They never chatted about who they were currently dating (no one for her right now), or about getting back together. They just connected so easily when they texted each other back and forth, as if they were friends. Friends who would never see each other again—his rule. She knew if she saw him she'd throw herself at him, beg him to take her back, and she was too proud to bring herself so low.

The wine glass was empty, as if by magic. She refilled it and continued sipping. Since this only happened once in very rare while, she'd pay for it tomorrow with a hangover. Hell, maybe she'd call in sick. She deserved a sick day, especially after that stupid, arrogant asshole of a doctor—

Her fingers flew over the keypad on her phone, texting Ian before she got herself into more of a downhill spiral.

Is it too late to talk? I'm drinking terrible wine. Wish you were here.

Ian replied a full five minutes later, as if hadn't had a response to that quite ready. Not surprising since she'd never even suggested breaking his rule before, at least not after the first year. They were supposed to be done with each other, but he wouldn't tell her why.

His text said: *Stop, Grace. you know we can't see each other.*

Grace glared at the phone. *Are you married? Did you get someone pregnant while we dated and that's why you jettisoned out of my life?* She misspelled the word jettisoned in her tipsiness, but autocorrect worked in her favor for once.

Grace waited for his response, knowing already what

he'd say. She'd asked him this before. He always told her that there was no one else, but he needed something more that she couldn't give him, and so he was moving on.

He'd even quit his job at the law firm, and never told her where he'd taken a position instead. All he ever made clear was that everything changed, and that included his relationship with her.

As in, there would be no relationship with her.

Grace poured herself another glass of wine, filling the cup to the top, which basically made it two glasses. Since drinking wasn't normally her thing, the first drinks has already taken hold of her around the edges, blurring the harshness of the day—and the harsh reality of what she knew Ian was in the process of texting her.

His text popped up on her phone. *I can't keep hiding who I am from you.*

She started to text back, to ask him what he meant, but another text from him came in first.

I pussy out telling you the truth because I don't want what little connection we still have to go away.

She gasped. Did he just come out of the closet to her via text? Wait, how was Ian gay? It didn't seem possible. Sure, he never seemed satisfied with their sex life, but…really? And he used the word *pussy*, not as a noun, but still quite out of character for the Ian she thought she knew.

I feel like an idiot, she replied. *I'm still your friend, even if you're gay.*

I'm not gay, he texted back. *I'm a Dom.*

IDK, she wrote. She didn't know what that meant.

This is me, his next said, next to a hyperlink. *I'm into BDSM. Still wish I were there? Or have I scared you off forever?*

Dom. BDSM. And a link that looked like something she might want to avoid opening on her smartphone.

TTYL, she replied, since her fingers were feeling too clumsy to type out 'talk to you later" and she knew he'd know what she meant. There was some research to do before she responded to him about things she knew nothing about.

So he finally had given her an answer. A real answer, after three long years of making her choose between infrequent texts that were always about her, never about him, or nothing.

The computer screen lit up as Grace logged on; she ignored the lure of Facebook and email. She opened a private browsing tab, because if anyone ever saw the things she was about to Google in her computer history, she'd die of embarrassment. She turned off the recommended "safe-search."

Grace hadn't even been sure what BDSM stood for until Google spelled it out for her. Bondage. Domination. Submission...or Sadism... and Masochism. People who got off on hurting others and on being hurt. It made no sense to her. Apparently, this was what some people did for a living, too. Get beaten for videos on a BDSM porn site—the hyperlink Ian had sent her.

The website filled her screen, a professional-looking set up with crisp photos of naked women, bound and gagged, with marks all over them filling the borders of the site. A big *Subscribe Now* pop-up obscured an obscene picture of a reddened ass.

Ugh. She didn't want to give these people her credit card. She x'd out the pop-up and saw a list of the videos available for immediate viewing...short clips, under ten seconds long, designed to entice the viewer to pay to see the whole thing. She clicked one that showed a still of a pretty girl's face, eyes wide, a ball gag in her mouth.

Slutty Nikki gets whipped with a vibrator tied to her pussy. Download now.

The fingers on her right hand seemed to click the mouse of their own accord, despite the dizzying lurch in her stomach at the sight of the image and its description. Or maybe it was the wine, since her overly-full glass was now empty. The clip played, showing Nikki bent over some sort of black ramp, a long white back massager attached to her upper leg with rope, the door-knob sized end of it pressed against the junction of her thighs. The vibrator.

A man came into the camera's view, but she could only see his arm—a lean, muscled arm clad in what looked like a black T-shirt. He was holding a whip.

Is that really Ian?

It looked like how she remembered Ian's arm, or maybe he'd been playing a joke on her when he texted her that hyperlink. Trying to trick her into watching porn, something she'd never done before.

The whip came down and a muffled squeal emanated from Nikki's mouth. The clip stopped. It had only been ten seconds, but Grace felt breathless, as if she'd been unable to take in air while the clip played.

Download Now, the pop-up said. *Download now for $7.50, a fifteen minute video of your favorite slut getting her ass whipped with a vibrator tied to her pussy.*

Grace shuddered. It didn't look consensual. It didn't look fun. She had to see, was that really Ian doing those horrible things? Was there anything in the whole video that showed that Nikki was really there because she…wanted to be?

Forget it. She couldn't watch fifteen minutes of that. Grace stood up and turned her back on the computer, stripping out of her scrubs as she headed toward the bathroom to change into pj's, her feet unsteady beneath her. Too much wine, but not enough. Not tonight. The scrubs went on top of yesterday's scrubs in her hamper, the pile of laundry getting to that almost-daunting spot where she'd have a hard time lugging the bag down the hall to the building's coin-operated laundry room.

If she watched the whole video, then she'd know for sure that it was—or wasn't—Ian. And if it was? Could she ever think of him the same way, knowing he was into such kinky stuff? He liked hurting women.

That must be why he insisted we never see each other again. He didn't want to hurt her so he got himself a job where he'd be paid to hurt other girls.

Yeah, there were other girls on that porn site, and what about them? Other women who could be getting hurt. Grace washed her face, staring at herself in the bathroom mirror. She had to at least know if that girl Nikki really was okay with Ian beating the hell out of her. If this website was operating out of South Florida, which it must be if it's where Ian went "to work", then her city must have dozens of other women getting roped into being beaten for money.

And if Ian was the man holding the whip—what then? Did he own the porn site?

Damn it. She hung the damp towel carefully back on its rung and stepped back into the living room. Her computer had gone to sleep, so no obscene images assaulted her. But she had to see. Had to know, to be sure.

Grabbing her credit card from the wallet she kept in her purse, she walked back over to the computer and sat down. The movement must have jostled the mouse, because the screen came to life as if by magic.

Now was her dinner time, but she wasn't hungry.

Download Now.

Grace took a breath and entered her credit card information, half-wondering if there was some sort of FBI watch on this website. Was downloading a video of a woman getting beaten illegal? It seemed wrong. Dirty.

A separate media viewer opened up and the video started playing. Nikki was talking to whoever was behind the camera, no ball-gag yet. When would she be gagged? The audio was terrible, but she could hear a flirty female laugh.

Nikki smiled at someone off-screen. The man who had been holding the whip stepped into the frame fully. *Ian.* Fuck, it really was him. Tall, with impossibly broad shoulders and a tight black T-shirt on, just like in the clip.

In her memories of him he'd always worn a button-down shirt and tie. Here, he looked sexy as hell and positively dangerous.

Ian had the vibrator—a long white vibrator with an electric cord attached to it—in his hand this time, no whip. Did Nikki know what she was in for?

Grace couldn't help but stare at Ian's face after not seeing him for so long. Handsome as ever, with a chiseled, clean-shaven jaw. His dark hair was clipped short. He seemed so... normal. Like he used to be. Not like a man who was about to leave the sort of marks on Nikki that Grace had seen in that ten-second video sample.

And that wasn't the worst of the samples. Some of those clips showed images of clothes pins clamped on nipples...and other places.

Ian might be the website's owner, or perhaps just another actor, playing the role of the Dom. But they weren't acting. It was real.

On Grace's monitor, Nikki was still smiling, chatting with Ian as he tied the vibrator to her thigh. Then she jumped a bit when he plugged it in and turned it on, her expression quickly becoming one of ecstasy. It was hard to hear them when they were just chatting quietly, since neither appeared to be wearing a mike, but Nikki's loud moans came through her speakers clearly as the vibrator buzzed. She turned the volume down on her computer, glancing at her thin walls for a second.

Her neighbors must think she was watching porn. Which...she was.

Ian came up behind Nikki and settled her over the black ramp, swatting her naked buttocks with his hand, several times, turning the skin pink. Grace squirmed in her seat, uncomfortable with the flutter in her belly as she watched. Her body betrayed her, her nipples tightening with unwanted arousal. The spanking looked...

(hot)

...fun, maybe. Like something she should add to her

bucket list.

I must be tipsy to even be thinking that. She shook her head, censoring her thoughts before they could get out of hand.

Why censor thoughts, though? They were just thoughts. It wasn't like she was doing anything other than sitting there, thinking. No need to censor thoughts about maybe, possibly, thinking a spanking might be hot.

How come Ian never tried to spank her? He'd never even suggested it. Although if he had, to be honest, there was no telling what her reaction would have been. Ian must have known she wouldn't be into it, or he wouldn't have broken things off with her so he could be free to find someone who shared his kink.

Grace poured the rest of the bottle of merlot into her glass, ignoring the splash of red on the tile floor. She could get it later, when the floor wasn't moving quite so much.

Clearly Nikki was having fun with the vibrator and the spanking, but what about the gag? The whip?

As if on cue, Ian left the screen and came back into view wielding what looked like a black leather whip, the same whip she saw in the ten second clip.

Nikki looked at the whip with desire in her eyes that Grace could see even through the video. Nikki licked her lips, but seemed caught off-guard by that first lash. A long red whip-mark lined her right buttock now. She moaned, then basically screamed as the whip came down again and again.

On the video, Ian paused. *"Have you had enough, slut?"*

Grace hadn't been able to make out their other words, but this sentence came out clearly, the word "slut" said almost as if it were an endearment. The word still grated on her, and she strained to hear Nikki's answer, half-rooting for her to tell him off, half-wondering what would happen if she did. Is that why he gagged her?

"No, Sir. Please whip me, Sir."

He brought the whip down on her flesh and Nikki

screamed again. The scream had a lilt to it, as if the sound was fueled by passion instead of pain. Maybe it was.

This time he smiled at her reaction. Still, he shook his head, dropped the whip, and came back with the ball gag.

Grace couldn't hear what he was saying, but it looked like he was asking her permission to gag her. He opened his hand twice quickly, as if showing her some sort of hand signal—perhaps a signal she could use if she needed to talk?

And then he gagged her. Nikki looked calmer, somehow, with the gag in her mouth, and she didn't hold back as Ian whipped her more, her sounds now muffled.

This part must be the ten seconds she'd seen in the preview. Nikki gagged, screaming against it, being whipped brutally. But now Grace could see the truth—she wasn't being beaten against her will. It was her job, one she appeared to get off on.

Just like it was Ian's job to torture her.

And from the looks of things, he enjoyed it. Obviously, he enjoyed it enough to choose BDSM over being with someone "vanilla"—another term she'd picked up from her frantic Googling—someone vanilla, like Grace.

Do vanilla people get a little turned-on watching their ex-boyfriend whip another girl?

Grace turned off the computer, too exhausted by the last fifteen minutes to deal with liking her friends' Facebook statuses or to answer emails from her mom about whatever new hypochondriacal illness she'd invented for herself lately. As the nurse, Grace got a lot of texts and emails from family and friends wondering if they could mix certain meds, if they had Lyme disease or ringworm, if they should use ice or heat, etcetera, etcetera, ad nauseum.

She laughed, the sound like a shot in the now-silent apartment. Who was she kidding, she liked it. At least then she got some respect for her skills, a respect she didn't receive from the doctor who employed her. Or from any of her past boyfriends, for that matter, other than Ian. Mutual respect—the one criteria in a partner she could never compromise on—was a trait sadly missing from her relationships.

At least in addition to the modicum of respect she got from her family for being an RN, nursing was most likely a better a way to earn a living than getting severely beaten. She laughed again, but it sounded weird in her ears. Too much wine.

It didn't make sense—the inexplicable desire that forced her body to betray her when she watched Ian dominate that girl.

How could Ian have changed so dramatically in three short years?

It was clear from the video that Nikki was getting more out of it than just whatever they were paying her to be broadcast on the internet.

But what about all those other girls? What else was Ian doing to them? The image of the clamped nipples from the website came to mind, and she felt a flush rise up her neck.

That had to hurt, right? Setting down her empty wine glass, she leaned back in her computer chair, her breath quickening. This was crazy. She slowly reached her hand up under her pajama top and pinched her left nipple. A rush of endorphins shot through her, and she pinched harder, holding the tension the way she imagined a clothes-pin or clamp would. Harder.

A line of sensation from her nipple went straight to her clit, causing a tingle down below without even touching herself there.

Oh God, what am I doing? Basically masturbating to internet porn. Unbelievable.

She pulled her hand out of her pajama shirt, sure she was red from head to toe. Her fair skin always betrayed her emotion by blushing, a trait she'd never appreciated. She supposed it went with the dark hair, although she'd rather be one of those tan Florida blondes than the pale sort she'd always been.

Taking a breath, Grace stood unsteadily. She'd start a load of laundry. It needed to be done anyway—

and it will give me more time to peruse the website

—so she may as well do it now.

No need to worry about her laundry being stolen from the laundry room at the end of the hall this late at night. No one cared about a bunch of dirty scrubs from Walmart.

Her body felt on fire and her left breast ached a little, a leftover reminder of how hard she pinched herself. There were more videos, more BDSM scenes, and she had to see them. Had to see more of Ian. He was like a drug to her, getting a little taste wasn't nearly enough. She'd never get tired of looking at him, even if she could only look at him online.

Tiny butterflies fluttered in her stomach as she returned from the laundry room and sat in front of her computer. She updated her Facebook status:

*Long day, good night everyone! *muah**

...and then logged out. It felt like she was giving herself an alibi almost, like if anyone happened to be wondering if she was looking at internet porn—scary, BDSM internet porn—she could point to that status and say, "Who me? I went to bed early!"

But...surely she wasn't the only one who watched these videos, right? They had to be making money from someone, and it wasn't just the $7.50 she gave them earlier to watch Ian's video.

Who else watched them? The thought of men, men like Ian, watching the videos and masturbating to the scenes of beautiful girls getting sexually tortured both scared her and...she paused, unable to even think the word.

(aroused)

She was wet though, she could feel it as she shifted position in her chair. Her body betrayed her now just like it did when she blushed.

One of the ten second preview clips showed Ian in the black T-shirt standing in front of a woman, a different woman, pulling her arms high above her head so she was forced onto her tippy-toes. He looked so familiar, his body, the way he moved. And yet the things he was doing were completely foreign to her.

I'd let Ian do that to me, just to feel his hands on me again. To be with him once more.

No, she was simply drunk and missed him, the usual result of any inebriation on her part.

What would he do next?

Download Now.

Grace hovered her mouse of the button, then quickly x'd out of it.

Another clip showed a woman with long dark hair in a ponytail lying on her stomach. The ponytail was attached by a band to…something inside the woman's anus. Oh my God.

Restrained by an ass-hook, Naughty Sara won't be released until she shows us how well she can suck that dildo. Download Now.

The alarm on Grace's cell phone went off and she nearly shrieked in surprise, the sound catching on her lips. She jumped up to put her laundry in the dryer, grateful for the break. Were all those women really doing this of their own free will? What if they were impoverished, and this was their only way to make money? Where they doing it for fun, for sexual kicks?

The thought of an actual metal hook being used to restrain someone seemed so…unsafe. Couldn't that perforate the rectum? The nurse in her couldn't help but be concerned, but whatever this website had awoken in her felt strangely curious.

And…

(aroused)

Grace shook her head and walked back down the hallway, setting her timer again to let her know when the laundry would be done.

She wanted to see the porn studio for herself. See the implements, see the cameras, see the women and…Ian. Just to be sure everything was the way it was supposed to be, according to the internet—all safe and sane and consensual.

Get real. That's not the only reason.

Okay. A small part of her wanted to see for herself because she thought it was interesting. And she couldn't get Ian out of her mind now that she'd seen him again, even if it wasn't in person.

I need to see him in person.

Her memories of Ian as a straight-laced lawyer, always the gentleman, always so proper, were nothing like the man who held the whip. She had to see it for real, to make it mesh in her mind. And to show Ian that he hadn't scared her off forever after all.

On the very bottom of the website, right next to their privacy policy, was a link:

Hot chicks click here.

Whether or not she was a hot chick was up for discussion as far as she was concerned, but the link took her to a page that gave an address only eighteen miles from her apartment according to Google Maps, and an email address to request an "audition."

Was she really going to do this? Grace took another sip from her glass before remembering it was empty. So was the bottle.

Oops. She hadn't meant to drink the whole bottle. That explained how she'd just spent over an hour watching hardcore BDSM porn. It was the alcohol, not her own interest. She giggled.

Don't lie to yourself, your panties wouldn't be wet if you weren't a teensy bit interested.

And not just in marching in and being the—the what?

The porno police, undercover as an auditioning porn star. Ha.

It wasn't for real. Right? It was just so she could get in, to see Ian in action for herself. She would go in and look around and tell them she changed her mind. She agonized over the wording of her email for twenty minutes, having to type very slowly and carefully since the letters on her keyboard weren't in their rightful places (or it could be the wine, either way) only to be answered by an auto-responder that said to come by Monday through Friday before shooting for the day began at 11am and to bring proof of her age and her social security card to prove she could legally work in the United States.

Easy as that.

That night she masturbated quietly, one hand beneath the sheets, visions of Ian's arm coming down on her, wielding a long, black whip.

CHAPTER TWO

An invisible band around Grace's chest tightened as she drove into an industrial-looking part of the city. Some houses with plywood over a window popped up here and there behind ragged lawns overgrown with weeds.

She'd called in sick at work, something she rarely did unless she actually had a fever or something contagious. All she had today was a red-wine hangover and…an audition to go to.

What would Ian do when he saw her again? Would he make her leave? He couldn't do that if she was there for a purpose other than to see him, right? Right. The audition. Maybe save some girls if they don't look as enthusiastic as that girl Nikki had been. No big deal.

The building was a squat-looking one-story concrete block, which fit in with the surroundings perfectly. All of the windows were covered on the inside with black so she couldn't see in, and she imagined it was how they helped control the lighting of the scenes.

Scenes. Porn. BDSM. *Ian*. What was she getting

herself into?

Since she had nothing that could possibly be deemed BDSM-gear to wear to her "audition", Grace chose a black tank top and denim shorts. Would they notice that her thighs were unmarked, that she'd obviously never done anything like this before?

Yeah, they'd notice. She'd be lucky if they didn't assume she was some kinda cop or narc. Especially since she was sort of going in there to check them out. See what Ian had gotten himself into.

Perhaps she should have called the cops to check them out. They could have gone in and made sure all the girls were happy and safe and Ian was still the good man she remembered, and she wouldn't be there, half because of that mission and half because of her own curiosity.

Curiosity killed the cat. She laughed to herself, sitting in her car with the doors locked and the air-conditioning running, because a very dirty thought crossed her mind. One that would never in a million years have crossed her mind before she started watching the porn videos.

Curiosity killed the *pussy*-cat. Pussy. Oh my God, she never used that word. Not during sex—not that she'd had any of that since the fiasco with Steve almost six months ago—and not anytime else. But now it came to mind as easily as if she was already an internet porn-star.

Okay. She was ready. Turning the car off, she stepped out into the thick humidity and heat. Her hair was probably going to frizz before she had a chance to walk inside, but that didn't matter. All the girls in those videos looked a bit...unkempt. Hard to stay perfectly coiffed when you're being whipped and teased and spanked. Especially by a man as good-looking as her ex-boyfriend.

Deep breath.

It was 10:30am, well before they were supposed to start shooting, but hopefully close enough that Ian would be there. They couldn't start without the man who held the whip.

She raised her hand and knocked on the door.

No sounds emanated from the building. Were they closed? She checked her phone again to make sure she hadn't gone crazy and that it really was a weekday before 11am. And she had the right address.

Well, she was in the right place, which probably meant that she had gone crazy after all. Grace turned around and headed back for her car.

"Can I help you?" a deep voice said behind her. A familiar voice. A voice she hadn't heard in person in over three years.

Her pulse pounded in her ears as she turned a little too quickly on the paved parking lot and stared into the doorway.

"Ian."

Yes, it was him. The man who held the whip.

Except he wasn't holding a whip now, he was *Ian*—the man who walked out of her life without looking back...now holding the door open. For her.

The man had become even more devastatingly handsome in the years since she'd dated him, his dark hair short but with just a hint of gel in it to give it style. How could it be Ian? The Ian she knew was so staid, so normal. A lawyer with a future. This man was pure sex, pure danger.

And yet, it was Ian.

"I thought I scared you off for good last night,"

he said.

"Jury's still out on that one," she admitted. "But—"

Blue eyes. Dark hair. And so tall…several inches over six feet at the very least. Her breath quickened at the sight of him, adrenaline pumping through her veins. She felt almost as if she'd already slept with this new, dominant Ian, since he'd starred in her masturbatory fantasy last night. Ironic since the sex they had together when they dated was very missionary and non-fantasy-inducing.

Seeing him now, it seemed clear why their relationship failed, despite their feelings for each other. Perhaps he left because he wanted to do things to her, whip her, hurt her…and he never breathed a word about it. He had let her go without even asking if she'd want to try his kink.

Grace stood rooted in one spot directly between her car and the studio. Between safety and security and something slippery and dangerous and unaccountably desirable.

"But you wanted to see for yourself." He looked different, taller perhaps. Like he didn't regret finally coming clean about his new career, his new life.

"I drank too much wine last night." She blushed. "I don't know why I thought it would be a good idea to show up. I—" Grace turned around helplessly and started back toward her car.

"You did knock, right?" Ian asked pointedly.

"I did." Screw it. Let him see he couldn't scare her off with…whatever it was he was into now. He had made a mistake leaving her with no explanation. Turning back to face him, she strode toward the door and stepped inside the studio before she could change her mind. "I didn't hear anything inside so I thought you were closed or something."

"The building is pretty well soundproofed."

Of course. That made sense. But… "Then why do you gag the girls?"

"Because," he said, standing over her, his muscles apparent under his ubiquitous tight black T-shirt. "It turns me on."

"Oh." The word came out like a gasp, not at all as she intended. She laughed nervously and tugged on the hem of her denim cutoffs, wishing she'd worn something less revealing. "I had no idea you were into this stuff when we dated."

"I never told you." He paused, as if he wanted to say more, but just shook his head. "Tell me the truth—are you here to see me, or to judge me?"

"I not judging you. At least, I'm trying not to. But you finally tell me after all this time that you left me for this—" she gestured around her, "I have a right to see what it's all about."

"Damn." He grinned and she laughed, getting a glimpse of the Ian she had come so close to falling for in the past. "I can't believe it's really you, here. You look good. Even better than I remember." He reached out his hand as if to brush away some stray hair, but pulled back at the last moment.

She pushed her hair back herself. "Thank you. You look good too. Different, though."

"Everything's different, Grace. And I suppose you do have a right to see what I'm about now."

"Why didn't you tell me sooner?" she wanted it to sound tough, like she didn't care really, but it came out quiet and almost plaintive.

"We have catching up to do, but now's not the

time," he replied. "Excuse the expression—but what's a nice girl like you doing in a place like this? Why not meet me for drinks?"

"You would never have done that," she reminded him.

"I might have reconsidered our rule about not seeing each other if you had responded to my text the same way you had responded when you thought I was gay."

She frowned. "What do you mean?"

"Before I could tell you I was a Dom, you texted me and said we were still friends—that you didn't care if I was gay. But when I said wasn't gay, that I was Dom, you...you didn't really respond."

"You didn't even give me a chance to decide for myself if I was...um, into whatever. BDSM."

His expression proved she was right about that. As far as he knew, she didn't belong in his world. Was there anything she could do to change that impression? Did she even want to?

"Grace, it's great seeing you again, but I'm at work. I can't rehash our relationship and the last three years without you in the next ten minutes."

Ouch. "I didn't only come to see you," she said primly. "After seeing what you did to those girls I wanted to meet them for myself—"

"I didn't do anything to those girls. We played together. It's not just me randomly tying up some unwilling person and beating on them. It's mutual. Safe, sane, consensual, got it?"

"Well then, are any of those other girls here?"

"Not yet. Ricardo's on a call in the back office, though."

"Ricardo?"

"The set manager. Don't get on his bad side—he and his wife own the business," he said, gesturing around the building. It looked like a dungeon, with several areas filled with different...stations?...for scenes to be played out. Various implements and bondage gear, ropes, gags, metal things that looked positively dangerous, hung on the walls near each area.

"Looks a bit different from when I used to visit you at work."

He laughed, flashing bright white teeth and the expensive orthodontia from his adolescence. He took her trembling right hand in his and held it, their first physical contact in way too long. She missed this...she missed him. But was it the old Ian she still held a flame for, or this sexy new one who sparked a new, hotter burn deep inside her?

"Being a lawyer was great training for this job, believe it or not," he said. "As the Dom for the scenes, I do a lot of negotiating, playing. I'm the one who—"

"Holds the whip," she finished for him. "Sorry. Didn't mean to interrupt."

"Grace, be straight with me. What on earth are you *really* doing here?"

"I'm checking on the girls to see if they want to be here."

"No, I don't think you are." His words were clipped. "You came to see me—but this is not the time or the place."

The flush rising through her meant she was blushing, she knew it. Damn. Plan C it was, then. "Well, then, I came to audition. Maybe. Can you show me around?"

Ian gave her an unreadable look. "You came to audition."

"Yes. Maybe. I don't know."

"Turn around."

"Wh-what? Why?"

His voice softened. "I want to see something. Turn around."

Grace obeyed, feeling like she was turning her back on a predator with long sharp teeth. Her heart fluttered in her chest in anticipation.

"Grab your ankles."

Grace's panties dampened at his words, and she started to slowly bend over, readjusting her purse over her shoulder. *Wait.* What was she doing? She stood up so quickly that as she whirled back around she swooned, reaching her arm out to steady herself—and feeling only rock-hard muscle as her hand landed on Ian's chest.

"Sorry," she said, but didn't move her hand. "Orthostatic hypotension. I mean, head rush."

Ian only smiled in return, gently removing her hand from his chest. "You're not submissive. You've never done this before, and we both know it. Maybe you are here to see the other women," he mused. "You don't look particularly hungry."

"Hungry?" The word slipped out even as she realized what he meant. He thought she needed money, or rather, he thought she didn't.

Just then the front door opened, letting in a rush of humid air and blinding sunlight, along with Nikki—the girl from the video.

Nikki blinked at Grace as if in confusion. "What's she doing here?" she asked Ian. "Is Ricardo hiring girls *again*? He knows I need as many scenes as

I can get."

Grace's mouth went dry. She hadn't planned this very well. "Um, hi Nikki. I know your name from your work. Very…nicely done. So…"

"What are you doing here?" she repeated, walking over to her.

"I'm…here to audition." Grace wished her voice could be as strong as Nikki's right then, but her words came out a near-whisper. "Or, I could help you find another job if you're not happy here."

"Let me get this straight," Nikki said, nodding over to Ricardo—the owner—as he emerged from his back office. "You want to 'help' the poor little cam-whore find a job but you think that you might want to give it a go? Really? Do I have *fucking idiot* tattooed on my forehead?"

Suddenly the full breadth of Grace's stupidity came crashing down on her. Who on earth did she think she was to barge into a place of business on an unasked mission to save someone who didn't want—or need—saving?

If that was all she wanted, she could have placed an anonymous phone call and had the place checked out by professionals. Grace wouldn't even know what to look for if she tried. What had she expected? That she'd walk out of here with a tattered group of beaten girls ready to go out into the sun and find "real" jobs?

It was clear that everything on the set was fine. Nikki did have a "real" job, and that job deserved her respect, just as Grace wanted to be respected for her work at the doctor's office.

"Y-you looked like you enjoyed working here," Grace said, her eyes down. "I watched the videos. I know what you do."

Ricardo clapped his hands twice, as if to gather their attention. He was shorter than Ian, but had a similar muscular build. He was dressed in a button-down shirt and tie, as if he had a business meeting to attend later. For all she knew, he did.

"Listen to me, young lady," Ricardo said. "We're an onboard, legitimate company, *capiche*? We jump through every single hoop we have to stay that way. But what we don't do is play around with spontaneous visits from Good Samaritans who have absolutely no idea about consensual BDSM play when they see it. I don't need you watching us shoot and then running to the cops with some bullshit about abuse or sexual slavery or whatever the hell you think it is we do down here."

"You tell her, Ricardo," Nikki chimed in.

Grace shrugged as if none of it mattered anyway, hoping they wouldn't notice her trembling hands. "That was never my intention. I'm very sorry for the intrusion. I'll just be on my w—"

"She said she came to audition," Ian interrupted. "I say we let her."

Nikki laughed. "You—audition? Do you even know what that means at a place like this?"

Grace shook her head.

"Well," Ian placed his hand on her lower back, right above where her shorts rested on her hips. "Would you like to find out?"

Yes. But the word hung on her lips, unspoken. Instead she stood very still, focusing all of her attention on the large, warm hand on the small of her back. Ian's hand. How could something so gentle make those marks on Nikki? On those other girls?

"Come over here," Ian said, leading her with an

almost imperceptible pressure from his fingers. She walked over to the empty area with him, attached to him it seemed, as if their bodies were fused in that one spot right above her low-rise cutoffs where he touched her.

Ricardo mumbled something and disappeared into his office, reemerging with a few papers and a pen attached to a well-used clipboard. "First I need to photocopy your driver's license and social security card for my records. Then I need you to sign this consent."

Grace dug the cards out of her wallet, realizing she'd been clinging to her purse this whole time like a drowning woman clings to a life raft.

Her father had taught her never to sign anything she hadn't read, so she ignored Nikki's loud sigh as Grace took her time reading over the three pages. Basically, she was signing her consent to be videotaped, that she wouldn't have any right to the videotape, and that it became the property of the website. They had the right to show it on their site for no further compensation to her if they wished.

"I can't sign this," she said.

Ricardo balked. "Well, there's the door." He raised his eyebrows, but Grace didn't move.

"Can't...can't I sign something saying I consent to be videotaped for the audition, but that you won't put the tape online unless we decide to...work together? Because you're not compensating me for the audition, right?"

Ian laughed. "Don't tell me she's the first one to read the contract, Ricardo."

Ricardo shrugged. "Fine." He took her pen, made a big X through the whole contract except for the part about her consenting to be taped and that she had no rights to the tape, and initialed it before handing it back to her.

"Thank you," she murmured, signing her name at the bottom and setting her purse down out of the way.

Ricardo took the contract and her ID from her. He flipped a switch, and the spot of floor where Grace stood lit up perfectly. Looking at the lights, she could see they were all pre-set and marked on the floor with tape. If anyone bumped into one, she supposed, they could easily re-light the scene without having to stop for more than a moment.

Ricardo grabbed his camera off of one tripod and attached it to the tripod already in place at her...station. She really needed to learn their terminology.

Why? This wasn't supposed to be real. What was she still doing here?

Ian stepped back, looking at her appraisingly.

Oh yeah. That's why. Ian.

She'd thought she'd fallen for the sweet young lawyer he used to be, but she'd never seen him like this before. Never seen his dark side. The Ian she'd thought she was done with had become, in the course of a wine-soaked evening watching online porn, the most intriguing person she'd ever known in her life. And gorgeous. Hot damn, he was gorgeous.

"Whenever you're ready, Ian," Ricardo said, checking the viewfinder once more before moving back.

Ian smiled at her, that bright white grin of his, and she smiled back without thinking about it. Is this why all those tapes start off with the girls smiling?

Probably. It was impossible to look at his smile and not give him one in return.

She took in a shaky breath.

"So, Grace, tell me why you're here." Ian spoke in a soft, commanding tone, one her body immediately responded to, as if he were speaking the words inside her head instead of from slightly to the right of the camera.

"Well, um, my…friend…told me about the website and I looked it up and found it interesting."

"That's it? Interesting?"

Arousing.

Grace's face heated up and she laughed nervously. "I couldn't help but wonder why all those girls seemed to like it so much."

"So you thought you'd try it for yourself."

"Yes." The word came out choked, as if against her better judgment.

Ian moved into her space, right next to her, probably because he knew exactly where he'd be in view on the camera frame. "What turns you on?"

You.

The whip.

You.

Grace shook her head and looked at the black rubber mats down on the floor, anything to avoid looking in those probing blue eyes of his.

"May I touch you?" he asked, and as soon as she did she knew the reason, because she often had to do it herself as a nurse—get verbal consent before doing something the patient—or in this case, the woman— might object to. It was a practical way of avoiding an assault and battery charge. Had that happened to him before? He was getting her consent on camera, no less.

"Yes." Saying *yes* gave her a heady thrill that tamped down the bubble of anxiety. Where would he touch her? What had she just consented to?

Ian stroked the top of her hair, carefully pulling it together into a low ponytail in his hands, and pulled down. She had no choice now but to tilt her head up until she gazed into his eyes.

"Do you like that? When I pull your hair?"

Her mouth was dry and she licked her lips, unsure what to say. He tugged gently again and stood over her, his face mere inches from hers. This was unlike any interaction she'd ever had with him in the past.

This is the real Ian.

"Yes," she whispered. "I like it."

"And what if I ask you to turn around and bend over for me? Will you do it, or will you be naughty like before?"

The word *naughty* tickled something deep within her, and she grinned up at him as he let go of her hair.

"So glad I amuse you."

Grace stopped grinning, although she was pretty confident that Ian was teasing her. "Um, what will you do to me if I...bend over?" she asked, hesitant once more.

"I'm still not convinced you're even willing to *pretend* to be submissive for the cameras, much less willing to take direction from me," Ian said. "Right now, I'm asking you to bend over because you wouldn't before."

She turned around, the heat from the lights warming her skin. Ian stood behind her again, but this time all she felt was the moisture between her legs and the butterflies in her stomach as she slowly bent down and grabbed her ankles.

Her hamstrings were going to remember this tomorrow. She wasn't as flexible as she used to be since she gave up Pilates.

Grace closed her eyes in anticipation, but had to open them again to visually steady herself. Ian stood silently behind her, and she supposed he was watching even though he didn't touch her.

"Are you going to…" *Spank me?* But she couldn't say the forbidden words out loud.

"Am I going to what?" he asked, amusement creeping into his voice. Curiosity, perhaps.

"Nothing," she muttered.

"Am I going to what?" he repeated. It sounded like an order, even though he hadn't requested anything of her other than an answer.

"…spank me?" she whispered, grateful the hair tickling her burning cheeks obscured her face.

"Do you want me to spank you?"

Oh my God. I'm going to melt into the floor and die of embarrassment.

But Ian didn't seem to think there was anything to be embarrassed about. His matter-of-factness about it all served to remind her that on a BDSM porn studio set, a spanking was the least of her concerns.

"I'm just looking at you, Grace."

The way he said, the desire in his voice…she no longer felt embarrassed. Instead she felt sexy.

"Don't move." He walked around her in a slow circle until the blood began to rush to her head, making her dizzy.

She gasped as he reached out and touched her

hip, a sizzle of heat from his fingertips on her cool skin. But that was it. Just one touch.

"Stand up slowly," he ordered, and she did, slowly enough that her head rush receded.

"Are you alright?" he asked, the concern in his voice made her smile, as if he had just wrapped her up in a protective blanket with his words.

"Yes, thank you, Ian."

Ian smiled back. "On camera—and in the bedroom—I prefer to be called Sir."

The bedroom? If only he'd told her that back when they were dating, maybe things wouldn't have ended so abruptly between them. But would the old Grace have even entertained the idea of playing kinky sex games? Probably not. It would have sent her running. But now...

"Yes, Sir." The words felt less foreign in her mouth than she expected them to. Perhaps because he'd made her call him Sir before, if only in her own twisted imaginings late last night, with her hand buried beneath her sheets.

Ian turned to Ricardo, who had been watching their exchange from behind the camera. "This one could be fun to train."

Ricardo's face lit up. "Yes! We could have a whole submissive training series, first-time virgin type shit. The subscribers will eat that up."

Grace picked up her purse. "So you want me?"

Ricardo nodded. "Yup. Pay is nine hundred bucks a shoot. You'll have to sign the proper contract, though, missy, no fucking around. You could start tomorrow."

"I have to work tomorrow." She'd make about two hundred at work. The idea of making nine hundred for just a few hours was staggering.

"Tomorrow night then. Ian? You up for an evening shoot?"

Ian nodded, the smile on his face seeming to hide some secret thought process that she desperately hoped was about her. Would he masturbate to the thought of her tonight?

Maybe he had a new girlfriend—it had been over three years, after all. He'd obviously moved on. Maybe Nikki was his girlfriend. The thought turned her stomach. She'd just barely reunited with the man, but she wanted him. And she wanted him to want her in return.

Grace turned to the boss-man. "If you're going to make a whole series around me and my lack of experience, I think I should be better compensated." She held her breath, wondering if he would call her bluff.

Ricardo laughed. "You sure you're not a lawyer like our Dom here?"

She glanced at the smirk on Ian's face and decided to pretend she had no idea what they were talking about. Everyone didn't need to know she was a part of Ian's past. "I want...twelve hundred a shoot."

"One grand and you don't dare tell the other girls."

Grace glanced over at Nikki, who was smoking a cigarette in the corner, reading a magazine.

"Why don't you just pay all the girls a thousand?" Grace asked, unwilling to let this man pit her against the others.

Ian laughed. "He already does, Grace. And now you're getting your fair share, everyone's happy, and

Ricardo's an asshole."

Ricardo shrugged. "I'll see you tomorrow night. Don't wear too much makeup. How old are you?"

"Twenty-seven."

"No. You're nineteen, Grace, got that?"

Grace didn't try to hide a look of disgust and walked out the door. So now she was the barely-legal virgin? Ugh.

What had she been thinking? There was no way she should go back, despite the allure of making in a day what took her a week to make as a nurse. What if someone she knew recognized her on the website, or what if she actually got really injured?

No, no one would injure her at that studio. It all appeared to be as Ian had promised—safe, sane and consensual. Still, that wasn't Grace's world. Would never—*could* never—be.

But the whole "audition" had been such a turn-on to her. This might be the only way she got to see Ian again—for more than a quick "let's catch up sometime" coffee, anyway. And it would be exciting to play out some fantasies...fantasies she never even knew she had. Now she had Ian's voice in her head, calling her naughty, tugging on her hair, asking her if she wanted him to spank her...

This was how she could be with Ian again, one more time at least.

Tomorrow night.

CHAPTER THREE

Grace's workday at the office seemed to drag on interminably, but it was five o'clock before she knew it—as if time had sped up at the last moment, rushing her toward her evening's video shoot.

She couldn't do it. Once someone's on the internet, they're on it forever. What if her future husband wanted to run for President or something? He'd be horribly embarrassed when those pictures of her surfaced. And they would surface, even if her real name wasn't attached to them. All the dirty laundry aired during a Presidential election.

Yeah, keep focusing on your future husband, the President of the United States of America. Because that's what's important right now. She shook her head, trying to get out of her self-defeating sarcastic funk.

Did she really think she could lead a double life, where no one knew she secretly made kinky BDSM videos for an online porn site at night, and be a nurse during the day? What would happen when she finally found a boyfriend? He'd never approve.

Unless the boyfriend was someone like, say...Ian.

Just the thought of him sent an endorphin rush

through her. What would he do to her tonight? What if she didn't like it?

More importantly, what if I do like it?

But she'd never done anything like this before. There was a very good chance she'd be completely turned off, hate it, and then what? Would she be forced to continue because of some stupid consent form?

No. It seemed like a legit place, as far as she could tell. She'd be okay. And if anything happened where she felt violated or God forbid, raped, anything at all, she'd get that place shut down so quickly it would make their heads spin. It's not like she was some drug-user coming in off the streets looking to make a quick grand or something. Grace knew how to take care of herself. So that settled it.

She'd be fine.

Grace set the office phones to the "night" setting, which forwarded them to the on-call emergency service that would page the doctor if one of his patients ended up in the hospital, and shut the lights.

Time to go get dominated by Ian. And who knows what else would happen.

*****

Grace had changed out of her scrubs and into her street clothes before she left work, and now waited at the studio in front of a wall of…implements, contemplating what they were for. Ricardo had suggested she wear cute cotton panties and a matching bra instead of the sexy thongs Nikki preferred, since Grace was supposed to be the young virgin. It creeped her out, but nineteen was more than legal, and she clearly had a woman's body, so actual pedophiles shouldn't be too interested in her. Hopefully. The thought of turning on a pedophile made her want to vomit.

But Ricardo assured her that his subscribers and viewers were fetishists who liked bondage scenes and light sexual torture and BDSM. The whole "nineteen-year-old virgin" thing was just an added fun bonus for them (especially since she was, in reality, a twenty-seven year old who'd had either four or five lovers, depending on how one defined "lover"). Ricardo said they always made sure to show the girls having fun so there was no question as to whether or not it was consensual. And they always gave a safeword and honored it.

Safeword. So much to learn. And a hand signal if she was gagged, which was something Ian had said turned him on.

And the thought of turning Ian on…well, that got her hot. Very hot.

Ian came up behind her, startling her out of her reverie. "I didn't think you'd come back," he said.

"Me either," she admitted, turning to face him.

He smiled and leaned in close, so close she half-expected him to kiss her.

"You don't have to do this if you don't want to, you know," he said, his breath hot on her ear. "As much as I'd enjoy training you, and would hate to see you go."

"Then why are you trying to get me to leave?" she whispered back.

"Because you don't belong here. You've always been such a good girl—at least you were back when we were together. I don't think you belong on a website such as this one."

Her heart sank to the pit of her stomach. As much as she didn't want to agree, Ian's words rang true because he was right. She didn't belong here, but it wasn't because she was a "good girl." She never should have come here in the first place. It wasn't the website that excited her, or the money, or the idea of being on the internet for thousands of viewers to watch and fantasize over.

It was just Ian. This new version of Ian who held the whip excited her, nothing more. Well…maybe more. More of the things he'd done to her during her audition. More of the way he made her feel…sexy, desired, controlled. Cherished.

Grace looked up into Ian's blue eyes, remembering the feel of his hands on her hair, tugging her head back until she was forced to return his intense gaze. She wanted more of that. But how, if not like this?

"Ricardo's not here yet," Ian advised. "I could text him that you never showed. He's home having dinner with his family, he won't care. He'll tell me to lock up and leave."

Grace took an uncertain breath. She had one last chance to make her decision to do this. A lot had changed in three years, and Ian was a different man now. Even if she desired him, was she willing to be on camera to have one last sexual experience with him? She glanced at the door. Flee? Stay?

"He'll be here any minute," Ian said. "Decide now, before he gets here. Do you really want your image to be on the internet, naked, in bondage, forever? What will your children think if they run across it?"

"I hardly think my future children will be looking at old porn websites, if they're even still around in twenty years," she scoffed, but the vision haunted her just the same. And the idea of her on the internet, naked and in bondage, did little to excite her sexually.

Damn it.

"Okay," she said. "You're right. Text Ricardo and tell him I never showed."

"Good girl," he said, pulling out his phone. His long fingers flew across the screen quickly, and he laughed. "Ricardo replied 'Shocker. Lock up for me.' Just like I knew he would."

Grace laughed and then looked around. It was dark out now, even though it was only around seven p.m. Only a few sections of the studio were lit.

"Thank you for saving me from making a dumb mistake," she said, picking up her purse.

"You're very welcome. Why are you picking up your purse?"

"Um…because you have to lock up and I should go home?"

Ian took a step toward her, a slight smile on his face that did nothing to stop the rush of adrenaline spiking through her. She felt like prey but in a really good way, somehow. Like she wanted to just lie down and let him…eat her like the predator he was.

Yes, Ian, you can eat me any day. She giggled nervously at her own thought.

"You don't have to leave," he said. "We have a whole playroom at our disposal. If you'd like, I can give you a taste of what you're so intrigued by. A taste of what brought you back to me."

Yes! This was how she could have her cake and eat it too. Or rather, have some alone time with Ian without committing to an internet porn-site and a three page contract. "But, just for us, right? Not for the camera?"

Ian nodded. "No cameras. No internet. Just us."

Us. How she missed his voice saying that, joining them with a single word. Every atom of her being wanted to respond with a resounding *yes!* but fear held her back. "I don't know," she whispered. "I've never done anything like this before."

"I'm not going to pressure you into something you're not ready for. You've never shown interest in BDSM before—and it was too much for me to hope that would suddenly change."

But she didn't move, didn't head for the door. All this time thinking about Ian, only to discover that the Ian she missed had been replaced by a new man. A very sexy man. She'd never desired him this much in the past, not like she did now. That had to mean something.

"I'm scared," she admitted.

"I'll walk you to your car, then. We can catch up over coffee sometime. It was…really great seeing you again, Grace."

It couldn't end, not like this. She wanted this. Why

fight it?

"Wait. I'll—I'll stay. Where do you want me? What do you want me to do?"

Ian smiled, a brief look of surprise passing over his face so quickly she wouldn't have noticed it if she hadn't known him so well.

"I like the sound of that," he said. "But first things first. We need a safeword."

"Okay. How about if I just say 'stop'? Or 'ow'?"

"That depends," Ian said. "Put your purse down."

She did, feeling shaky already, heady with excitement. Ian stepped in toward her, his physical strength and power so apparent as he stood millimeters away from her body, his body heat coming off of him in waves.

"It depends on your fantasy," he continued. "Do you have a fantasy of being hurt, of saying ow, of saying stop, and of having no control over what happens next? Do you want to be spanked until you cry, until you're beyond begging, and I decide you've had enough?"

She'd never thought that might be a fantasy before, but his words made her wet.

"Your hesitation indicates those might not be good safewords for you, then," he laughed. "Pick another."

"I don't know. I can't think straight. What's a good safeword? What do the other girls say?"

Ian took her hand in his, running his thumb over her pounding radial pulse in her wrist. "Let's get one thing straight. You are not those other girls. I'm not getting paid to be here with you. I'm here with you tonight for pleasure—for you, and for me."

"Okay." It gave her a little thrill to know he thought of her as separate, as special.

He pulled her against his body, and she could feel his erection through his jeans. Their conversation was turning him on as much as it turned her on.

Oh my God. Were they going to have sex? She hadn't planned on having sex. Not tonight. Not on their first date since they split up.

"Is this a date?" she asked, uncertainly.

"Do you want it to be?"

Grace laughed, uncertain, and not feeling up for inevitable rejection. "No."

"Good. I haven't been the dating type since we broke up anyway."

Oh. Of course. Disappointment crashed through her, but what did she expect? That the man who broke her heart so he could whip women on the internet for a living was going to take her out to dinner and a movie?

"Can I just say 'safeword', then?" she asked.

"Yes. Safeword is your safeword. Good idea." He grinned and stepped back, appraising her.

"Now what?" she asked.

"Now you learn patience, and you start addressing me as Sir."

She swallowed around the lump in her throat. "Yes, Sir."

Was this really happening?

"Take off your shirt, Grace."

She peeled it off, holding it tightly in her hands as if she could transfer some of her energy into it to calm herself down.

"Bra too."

The clasp in the back had never given her a problem before, but she fumbled with it until the cotton material slipped off her shoulders. Now she stood completely topless before him, wearing only her panties and denim cutoffs and flip-flops.

Grace heard a sharp intake of air. Ian was looking at her with an appreciative expression. "Grace, you are very beautiful. Very, very beautiful."

She dropped the clothes to the rubber mat below her and fought the urge to cover her breasts with her arms. Not that she was embarrassed of them—he'd certainly seen them before—but he was staring at her body with such…possessiveness and intensity she felt overwhelmed.

"I'm going to touch you, Grace," he murmured. "I'm going to play with your pretty little pink nipples."

Images of him putting clamps on that other actress's nipples flashed before her eyes, and she moaned with desire as he cupped her breast with one large hand.

Either his hand was very warm, or her skin was very cool, but it felt like a gentle heat surrounding her breasts as he took his time touching her, massaging her, running his hands along the curves of her cleavage and the fold under her breasts where they hung heavy on her chest.

"I like these nipples," he said, taking one in each hand. He pinched both gently at the same time, very lightly, and desire coursed through her body. It was as if there was a direct connection between her nipples and her clitoris, which swelled with arousal inside her panties.

She squirmed under his fingers, aware of the effect he was having on her…down there. Her pussy. Even thinking the word felt taboo and yet oh so right with Ian's fingers locked down on her tender nipples, now hardened little buds.

He pinched harder and she gasped in pain.

"Breathe," he commanded. "Breathe into the pain and let it turn into pleasure."

She hadn't realized she'd been holding her breath until she obeyed, filling her lungs with oxygen, and the pain centered in her nipples flowed through her body in a rush of sensation that left her feeling giddy and high.

"Keep breathing." He kept his grasp on her nipples tight, not letting up on the pressure for even a moment, although surely only a few moments had passed, even if it seemed like an eternity.

Ian pressed his body closer to hers, his denim-clad thigh between her spread legs. She ground her hips, rubbing her clit against his muscular thigh without shame as he continued to pleasantly torture her breasts with his long hard fingers.

"Like a bitch in heat," he whispered. "That turns me on. I want you to come, Grace. Rub your little clit on me till you come."

Her breath hitched and she moaned, the sensations building in her, and suddenly he let go of his hold on her breasts, flooding the nerve endings with a new level of erotic pain when the blood came rushing back into her nipples. She came hard, bucking her hips against him, gasping for air as her whole body convulsed with the strength of her orgasm.

Ian lifted her chin and kissed her, a deep, powerful kiss, thrusting his tongue inside her mouth. She would have fallen over if he hadn't been holding her so tightly.

"Do you usually kiss the girls?" she asked breathlessly.

"No, I don't. But I'm not working right now, am I?"

"No, Sir." She stood on her tip-toes and offered her lips to him again, but he just smiled down at her.

"You're going to be sore tomorrow," he said. "You might want to put some ice on those nips tonight before bed, maybe take some ibuprofen or something."

"Really?"

"Well, you're the nurse, so you can decide for yourself. That's just what Ricardo usually says to the girls after certain scenes."

"Wow. Okay. Dare I ask what sorts of scenes?"

Ian shrugged. "Anything where something could get sore. If you're not used to butt-plugs, for example, you might hurt the next day. A hard paddling will definitely make you sore, especially if I pound the muscle." He squeezed her ass through her cutoffs as if to emphasize his point.

"Do you...like hurting women?" Grace wasn't sure what the right answer was. Part of her wanted to hear him say no, that it was all just a job to him. Part of her wanted to hear him say yes, and say it in such a way that she could easily leave him, leave the fantasy behind and go back to her normal world where an orgasm didn't come with a heavy dose of nipple torture.

And part of her wanted to hear his explanation. Because surely, his erection didn't lie. He was turned-on. But what exactly about what just happened turned him on?

"Well," he paused, and leaned back against the black-painted wall. His cock was still hard, straining against his pants. "I wouldn't be able to do this job if I didn't love it."

"But why? How?"

"I'm sorry, Grace, I can't think straight when I'm in this state," he laughed, stroking his cock through his jeans.

She licked her lips. What did he want her to do? The few times she'd attempted to give him a blowjob back when they were dating she'd gagged her way through the whole thing, until he finally stopped asking. "I—I can't do that, Sir."

"Do what?"

"Fellatio." Her face burned and she looked down at the black rubber mat in embarrassment.

"We'll work on that, then. But not tonight." He unzipped his pants, revealing a thick, hard cock worthy of any porn movie. It looked bigger than she remembered it, perhaps because he was harder than he'd ever been for her before, perhaps because his dark pubic hair was clipped short and well-groomed. Although…she'd never actually seen his pants down in any of the videos on the website. He never had sex on tape with those women—she would have remembered seeing his cock like that.

"You only ever tie them up," she whispered, and he wrapped his large hand around his cock, stroking it firmly. "You don't fuck them. You whip them. Spank them."

Her words were having an effect on him, she could see. He stroked himself faster, staring into her eyes as she spoke.

"Why do you like to hurt those girls, Ian?"

"It turns me on," he said, his voice soft, as if half of his concentration were on her voice and the other on his hand moving swiftly over his cock. "The moans, the look of exquisite erotic agony uniting with pleasure, that moment when the girl thinks she can't stand it for a moment longer but then she does...and I reward her."

His breathing got faster and he groaned. "I love the power of it, of a woman bound and at my mercy. I can do whatever I want." He climaxed, a thick jet of come that looked like sugar-icing covering his hand. Ian looked down into her eyes and exhaled slowly.

"Thank you for being honest," Grace said, picking her bra and shirt up off the floor. She didn't know how she felt. Aroused still, but disturbed. It was clear he liked to dominate women, at least during sex. She'd grown up her whole life as a strong woman, so where did that put her?

And pain. He loved inflicting pain. But...there was something frighteningly familiar about his sentiments. Because everything that he said turned him on, turned her on as well...except, well, backwards. She wanted to be tied up. She wanted to be at Ian's mercy, so that he could do whatever he wanted to her.

"Excuse me, I need to clean myself up," he said, and walked past her and across the studio into the restroom. She heard water running and the toilet flush and the water run again as she dressed.

Alone in the...dungeon, which was basically what the porn studio was—Grace looked around and saw kink all around her. She didn't belong here, not if she was the "good girl" Ian seemed to think she was. Her breasts ached. Ian was right, she'd need to ice them and take an anti-inflammatory soon.

She picked up her purse. Now that she'd been with Ian again, now that he'd shown her what it was about, maybe she could go home and not wonder about the man who held the whip...about Ian, and what could have been.

Right?

"There's something you should know," he said from

behind her, and she whirled around, feeling guilty, as if he caught her planning an escape without saying goodbye.

"You don't owe me an explanation," she said. "I appreciate that you stopped me from working for the porn site. I really do. That would have been the stupidest move ever for me. And I also appreciate the…the lesson."

"What turns me on the most is knowing that you're turned on," he interrupted. "That's what you need to know. I don't fantasize about punching a girl in the face. I don't want to make her bleed, or break a bone or do anything that would actually hurt in a non-sexual way. I like sadomasochism, but only if I have a true masochist—a pain-slut—to play with. I'm not violent, not at all."

"You're a lover, not a fighter," Grace said, bemused.

Ian shrugged. "I just didn't want you to get the wrong impression of me. I know what it looks like on those video downloads. But still—you came here for a reason."

"I wanted to see if we had that old spark, I suppose."

"We don't," he said.

Grace's eyes stung with his declaration. How could he say that? Tonight's experience had been electrifying, at least for her. Apparently not for him, however. "I should go home. I have to work in the morning."

Ian nodded, his handsome face unreadable. "We don't have the old spark because there never was a true spark before. Not like tonight. Tonight, you lit me up in a whole new way. I'd like to see you again."

"On a date?" she asked, wanting to feel the sting of rejection now—so she could more easily walk out the door.

"No, that's not where I am right now. We can't jump back in time to the same relationship we had before, because that one didn't work out. But I think you had a good time tonight, and if I'm right, then maybe you'd want to play some more."

"What would you do to me?" she asked. Why couldn't she turn around and leave already? Was she such a glutton for punishment?

"Whatever I wanted."

A spike of lust ran through her. *Yes.* "I don't know…"

"I have keys to the studio. I'll meet you here tomorrow after work. My whipping arm might be tired from shooting all day, but I'll save some energy to spank you. I'm dying to see that ass of yours turn pink under my hand."

Grace flushed, and she knew her cheeks were turning as red as Ian would probably make her bottom if she dared to show up tomorrow.

Do I dare?

She walked out of the studio on shaky legs, not knowing the answer.

*****

Ian waited until she'd exited the studio door before watching from the side of the black curtain that covered the front window to make sure she got into her car safely. She sat in the car with her headlights on for a moment, perhaps setting her GPS?…before pulling out and leaving his Jeep Wrangler alone in the parking lot.

There was something special about Grace, always had been. If when they were dating he had heard those breathy moans of desire as he pinched and played with her, he might never have left. He'd always cared about her—one of the reasons he continued texting with her long after they'd broken up. It was one way to keep a part of Grace in his life.

Ian hadn't meant to tell her the truth that night she texted him, but when she suggested he come over, the urge to comply, just to see her face again, was so strong that he had to know what she thought of his lifestyle. She needed to know exactly who she was inviting into her home—and it wasn't the man she thought she knew from their time as a couple three years ago.

She'd always been so conservative, so demure. Girls

like that didn't walk onto his set, ever. The actresses Ricardo usually hired knew their way around a BDSM scene and weren't afraid to flaunt it. They got off on exhibitionism as much as they got off on the BDSM aspect.

Grace didn't seem like the exhibitionist type. Not with the way she kept blushing. She didn't play to the camera during her audition, or try to woo Ricardo into liking her as the other girls did, since he was the head honcho. Ian was just a hired hand, really. The whipping hand.

And he didn't feel even an ounce of guilt over lying to Ricardo about Grace not showing up to protect her from tarnishing her image permanently. Some girls loved having their face and tits, bound up tight, all over the internet. They wanted to be seen whenever someone Googled with the safe-search off, being used and sexually tortured for their own pleasure as well as the viewers.

But not Grace. Grace didn't even know what she wanted, which was attractive in its own way. Like Ricardo said, she could be the nineteen-year-old virgin type, except she wasn't. She knew enough about what she wanted to have the guts to actually come down to the studio and see him. To audition. To bend over for him...

Fuck. His cock went to half-mast, already aroused again. It was thinking of Grace that did it. Grace obeying him, doing what he said...and he could tell that she loved every second of it. She'd humped his thigh till she came, for God's sake. This was no virgin.

But she needed training. If she was willing, he'd love to be her Dom...at least for now.

She'd mentioned dating more than once, which seemed to indicate that she still wasn't the type who was interested in a purely sexual relationship. It was all he knew since he left her, though.

I'm not the boyfriend type. If I've learned anything over the past few years, it's that.

But did it have to be that way, forever? He'd have to change paths at some point, why not now, when he finally reunited with someone that stirred his emotions as well as his cock?

Ian turned off the lights and locked up behind him. He sat in his Jeep for a few moments himself, taking the time to relive the past hour he'd spent with her. The best hour of his day. Hell, best hour of his year, maybe.

If she came back tomorrow, he'd have to give her what she was looking for to keep her coming back for more. Because Ian wasn't ready to lose sight of Grace just yet.

He grinned into the night.

You don't know it yet, Grace, but after tomorrow night, you're going to be thinking of me every time you sit for the next week.

CHAPTER FOUR

Grace watched videos of Ian for almost an hour before going to bed. Who needed television when she had bondage porn starring the sexiest man she'd ever met? And to think when they dated in the past, she merely thought of him as handsome, but not sexy per se. It was his dominance shining through, and his newfound self-confidence that made him exude sexuality now.

One clip she watched over and over before deciding if she wanted to download the whole thing. It showed a close-up of a woman's pussy as Ian slowly inserted his entire fist, one finger at a time. The full video was long, almost half an hour, because Ian took his time doing it. The video was well-edited, as all the ones on Ricardo's site were, alternating shots of the woman's face as she begged and moaned and orgasmed around Ian's large hand with shots of his thick wrist sticking out of her pussy.

That could never be her. If that was the sort of thing Ian wanted to do, then she was out, because how could she do something like that?

Well, women have babies, don't they? With heads bigger than a fist?

She shuddered. There was nothing hot about that.

Yuck. But she watched the whole video, just the same. The shots all focused on the girl, on her face, her writhing, her pussy with the wide wrist sticking out of it. But Grace wanted to see more of Ian than just the few shots where he was behind the actress.

Those were her favorite videos...the ones where he came behind a woman, bound with her arms above her head, and stood behind her, whispering in her ear as he ran his hands over the curves of her body. She knew he was standing in the shot that way to give the viewer the best access to the girl's body, to see it in all its naked, beaten and caned glory, but that was almost the only time Grace got to see Ian's face.

He'd made it perfectly clear that he had no interest in dating her again, which was almost definitely a blessing in disguise. She couldn't dare risk her het heart again on Ian, much less date a professional Dom when she was a self-professed vanilla gal all the way. No way. She was meant to find a nice normal guy and settle down, have kids, a dog, whatever. Soon, too, since she would be thirty in a few years. The two lives couldn't coexist, certainly.

Having a Dom in her life would just get in the way— even if it was Ian— because while she should be volunteering at the soup kitchen or going to church or doing the bar scene or whatever the hell it was a girl like her was supposed to do to find The One, she'd be in his dungeon, getting her fantasies played out for her, one by one.

Fantasies she never even knew she had until he told her she might have them.

Like when he suggested saying "stop" and him not stopping might be a fantasy. It seemed so...rape-y and weird. But it was true, that got her hot, at least the thought of it did. If that fantasy were played out in real life, would she be scared?

But she knew Ian, knew that he was genuinely good inside, and that she could trust him. While she couldn't trust him not to break her heart again, she could definitely trust him to respect her boundaries, and her safeword, "safeword." She giggled as she closed the computer for the night. Really? She couldn't come up with anything more original than "safeword" as her safeword?

He must think she was a complete moron. Or not, since he said he wanted to see her again, even after three years of avoiding seeing her in person. Her breasts ached, and even her sleep shirt seemed to rub irritatingly against her sore nipples. She popped some pain medicine and climbed into bed with her shirt off and the blankets down around her waist, letting only the breeze from the ceiling fan touch her tender nipples.

Could she be in relationship with a man who only wanted to pleasure her with pain? A man who would never take her to dinner, who would never sleep beside her in her bed? That's the sort of thing they used to do, and look how that turned out. She'd bored him straight out of the relationship and into a kinky new career path where he didn't have to make small talk before tying someone up.

She fell asleep knowing she couldn't be happy in a purely sexual relationship—not with Ian, not with their history—but that she'd still show up at the studio tomorrow after work. This was her one chance to get a spanking and she wasn't going to miss it, even if it meant saying goodbye to Ian would be that much harder.

She couldn't fault him for being honest just because she didn't like his answers. Even if there was a part of her—a part she'd previously hidden so deep inside her she never even knew it existed— that was struggling to the surface. The part of her that wanted to be at Ian's mercy once more.

*****

"I wasn't sure you'd show up," Ian said, opening the door for her to enter the empty studio the following evening.

He looked gorgeous, as usual. He also looked like

he'd gone home and showered and then come back.

"Do you still live in the same condo?" Grace asked, stepping inside and setting down her purse. She hadn't bothered to change out of her scrubs, preferring to come straight from work before she could talk herself out of it.

"Too expensive once I quit law. Now I don't live too far from you, actually."

"So you looked at my driver's license when I gave it to Ricardo, huh?" Was that weird, or cute? She couldn't decide.

"You know me, I can't help but look at anything with words on it. I can't help it, I have a photographic memory."

"I still don't believe you about that!" Grace laughed but Ian just shrugged and raised his eyebrows as if he didn't care if she believed him or not. Huh. Maybe he really did have a photographic memory? He'd mentioned it in passing before, but she'd shrugged it off as a bragging. She'd only ever read about that before...usually people who claimed to have one really just had good visual memories, but couldn't take an instant visual "picture" they could then go back and look at in the recesses of their mind.

Another interesting tidbit about Ian. She hadn't believed the old Ian, but this new one didn't seem the bragging sort.

"What's my middle name?" she challenged.

"That's too easy. I already know it's Francelle. If you're going to test me, test me."

"Okay. Um...what's my driver's license number?" Even she didn't know that by heart.

He closed his eyes briefly, more of a long blink, as if he were looking at the back of his eyelids for the answer, and said a string of numbers.

Huh. "Hang on." She reached back into her purse for her ID. "You're right. Wasn't expecting that."

He either really did have a photographic memory, or

he spent way too long staring at her ID. A hidden talent or a hidden desire to know as much about her as he could? Both possibilities intrigued her.

"I'm glad you came. I like being here, on neutral territory," he said.

"It's not neutral for me. This is your scene. Your...implements." She stuck her driver's license back in her purse. "Neutral would be a coffee shop or something."

He looked amused. "You want me to spank you at a coffee shop?"

"No. God no." Her face heated up and she knew she was blushing again. "So, um...what do we do now?"

"Now you strip. All the way. No doctor's office uniform, no panties, no socks. I want you completely naked."

Grace stood, rooted to the spot.

"You don't want to make me wait, Grace, not when you're about to get your very first spanking from me."

"From anyone, Sir," she whispered, and stepped out of her white nursing shoes, balancing precariously on one foot as she peeled off each sock.

"Not even for fun, a little quick smack on the ass as you walked by a boyfriend perhaps?"

"No, Sir. There haven't been any real boyfriends, not since you...Sir." She stepped out of her scrub bottoms, leaving her panties on, and pulled the top over her head.

"So you have absolutely no idea what it feels like to get spanked?" Ian asked. It was a tone that said he didn't believe her, and he was right not to.

She flushed and started undoing her bra and stepping out of her panties, hoping to distract him from his line of questioning.

"Tell me the truth, Grace," he said, a soft smile playing across his lips. "Tell me the truth and I'll go easier on you than if you lie to me."

This is so embarrassing.

"Okay, the truth is...after I watched some of your

videos of you spanking those girls, I...I got a wooden spoon from my kitchen and hit my own butt with it. Once. Like a moron, okay? I spanked myself." She burst out laughing, a nervous laughter she couldn't control because it was the only thing keeping her from running out of there in embarrassment.

Did she really just admit to that out loud? To Ian, of all people. The one person she most wanted to seem sexy to. Now all he was going to be able to think about when he looked at her was a silly woman standing in her kitchen, spanking herself with a wooden spoon because she wanted to see what the big deal was.

"Nice," he said, chuckling. "I like that."

"Yeah, right."

"No, I really do, Grace. Because it tells me that you've got a masochistic streak in you, and you know how much that turns me on."

She dared to glance up at him, her cheeks burning. "Really?"

"Really. Now let me show you how it's really done. You're not ready for a spoon, but I've got a very hard hand for you."

Without her panties on, Grace had to wonder if her arousal would become as evident as his. Would her wetness drip down the inside of her thighs if he kept talking to her like that?

"We have a spanking bench for you to lean over, but I think I'd prefer to do this the old fashioned way," he said, sitting down on one of the metal folding chairs that adorned the set. "Come here, over my knee."

Oh my God. This is happening. She looked at his legs warily, unsure of how to lay herself over his lap without falling off or being clumsy.

"Very well," Ian said, and he stood up, grabbed both of her wrists with one of his hands, and sat down again, pulling her over his lap.

She gasped. So much for doing this gracefully. There

was no way she'd fall off, at least, not with the firm grip Ian had on her waist. Her bare ass felt extraordinarily exposed. She imagined he was looking at it, inspecting it, and she squirmed uncomfortably at the thought.

Ian laughed. "I haven't even touched you yet. Do you remember your safeword?"

"Yes, Sir. I'm okay."

"You're more than okay, Grace," he said, rubbing her bottom. His hand felt so warm against her cool skin. "You're absolutely beautiful."

Grace smiled at the rubber-mat covered floor, even though he couldn't see her face. It was nice to feel beautiful, especially in such a vulnerable position. No one had ever seen her ass that close up before. And he kept rubbing her skin, kneading it with his palms as if her butt cheeks were dough.

Every second that passed as he held her over his lap without spanking her seemed an eternity. The anticipation made her woozy with desire. The thick length of Ian's erection poked into her belly, reminding her that she wasn't the only one getting something out of this experience.

Spank me.

"I'm going to warm you up," he murmured, as if he'd read her thoughts. "And once I think you're ready, we'll start for real."

She tensed, but nothing happened.

"Say: 'Yes, Sir.'"

"Yes, Sir."

With that, he brought his hand down on her ass, lightly at first, sending tingles of pleasure-pain that was almost pure pleasure through her. He patted both cheeks all over, warming her skin until heat seemed to radiate off of her. The sting was getting stronger now, and she squirmed again on his lap.

"What a beautiful pink shade your ass has now. Are you ready, Grace? I want to spank you properly."

"Yes, Sir."

The smack came hard and fast, taking her breath away with the sudden streak of pain. Without giving her a moment to catch her breath, he spanked her other ass cheek, then both, over and over, until all she could think about was his hand and her bottom and how *this* was what it meant to be spanked.

The idea of it was much sexier than the reality. The reality hurt, a lot. There was a reason it was used as a punishment, and Grace could see why. She'd rather be anywhere at that moment than under his hand.

Ow. Ow ow ow. Oh my God, someone remind me why I signed up for this. This spanking would last forever. She could use her safeword. Maybe she should. But instead she breathed, hoping the pain would flow through her and turn into pleasure.

And then, he stopped.

Grace looked up at him in surprise. "That really hurt."

"It's meant to hurt. It's a spanking."

"But…"

"May I?" Ian asked, and Grace nodded, having no idea as to what she was agreeing. She couldn't think straight, all of her energy was focused on the pain and on Ian, the man who had obvious erection from giving her that pain.

"Ah yes," Ian murmured appreciatively. He slid his fingers inside her pussy, and only then did she realize just how wet she'd become. She was dripping with arousal, the insides of her thighs were shiny and slick with it. She'd left a wet spot on Ian's khaki pants. "It may have hurt, but you liked it."

"Yes," she admitted, because the proof was there for them both to see. She'd have been embarrassed if it was anyone but him. At least with Ian, she knew that he was turned-on by the fact that she practically came all over herself from a hard spanking.

"You have the perfect ass for spanking," he said with a smile. "I've been fantasizing about doing that to you since we first started dating." He rolled her over on his lap and sat her up so she sat on her sore bottom, the bare skin rubbing against the canvas-like material of his khakis. He kissed her lips and slid his hand back between her thighs again.

"I wish you'd told me back then. We've wasted so much time—"

"You weren't ready for it then like you are now. You took your first spanking so well," he said, finding her clit. "I'm so glad I was the one to administer it."

Grace tried to focus on breathing, but soon her whole world narrowed again, and became Ian's fingers rubbing hard, tight circles against her clit. She didn't hold back as she moaned, trying to get more contact with his fingers. He sped up the rate and her womb clenched, convulsing as she climaxed right there on his lap. His embrace was both comforting and restraining—the strength he surrounded her with suggested he'd give as much pleasure as pain, whether she liked it or not—a thought that brought her climax crashing down on her. Moving her hips with abandon, she twisted in his arms, secure in the knowledge that Ian would keep her safe as he took her to the peak and back.

Ian slipped his fingers out of her and held them in front of her face so she could see they were slick and shiny. "Do you know what you taste like?"

The thought had never crossed her mind to find out. Why would she want to? But then Ian slowly pushed his fingers past her lips, invading her mouth, and she sucked instinctively, licking her juices from his hand.

"You must taste delicious," he said, watching her as she continued to lick his fingers, running her tongue over the tips.

This was nice, the invasion, the way he violated her mouth. She wanted more of that, more of the surrender, but that didn't make sense. There were no words to tell him that, or no words that she knew of. So she just kept sucking his finger, grinding herself on his lap.

He laughed as if he knew what she wanted, what she needed. "Okay. Get on your knees between my thighs."

The rubber mat was kind on her knees, and she sat back on her haunches, looking up at him. He really was incredibly good-looking. If he wasn't a porn-site Dom he could be a movie star or something. Men this good-looking didn't usually exist in her world—it was almost as if he'd become hotter since she knew him. Remove the straight-laced business-suited veneer and find a dangerously sexy Dom with a penchant for whipping girls in bondage.

How strange that here she was, on her knees completely naked, and he was fully dressed sitting on a chair.

If anyone she knew saw her now they'd think she'd gone completely mental. But the door was locked, the cameras were off, and it was just a little consensual fun between…whatever they were. Old friends? New lovers? No one ever had to know. It was her secret.

Ian unzipped his khaki pants and slid them down his thighs, freeing his cock from the black boxer-briefs he wore beneath. The tip was almost purple and shiny with pre-come.

"I thought you couldn't do this," he said, his blue eyes staring into hers.

"For you, I can. At least, I want to." She looked at his cock with longing. "I really want to try, Sir."

Ian smiled at her and she held his gaze as she took the head of his cock past her lips. He tasted like salty sex, like her own juices had tasted, but with a hint of his own masculine musk.

She put some suction into it, covering her teeth with her lips as she pulled more of him into her mouth.

"You're a pro, Grace. Someone has taught you well in

my absence. I'm almost jealous enough to spank you again."

A pro, huh? She laughed, the sound muffled by his cock, and continued doing everything she'd read about and seen online from the woman who sucked off the dildo to get out of bondage, on this very same porn-studio set. Even pretending to know what to do made it easier, although she honestly had no idea what to do about his testicles, so she avoided them.

"I want to stand up," he said, and she pulled herself off of him reluctantly, but stayed on her knees. "Good girl. Now I can fuck your mouth."

Those words, that's what she wanted. She just didn't know before. Ian took her face in his hands and slowly entered her mouth, sliding his cock over her tongue, reaching farther and farther down the back of her mouth with each thrust.

"Relax your throat, don't gag," he warned, and she tried to do just that as he thrust deeper into her mouth, faster, in and out. "You are so fucking sexy, Grace."

She sucked hard and he let go of her hair, pulling out just in time to come all over her neck and breasts. It splattered like warm water on her skin.

He rocked back on his heels with a groan and pulled his pants back up. "That was incredible. Don't move, I'm going to clean you up."

"Yes, Sir." She stayed still as a mannequin, kneeling on the floor, feeling the tickle of the come dripping down her chest. Now that she had nothing else to focus on, she realized that her ass was still burning. If she looked at it in a mirror, would there be red handprints on her skin?

She hoped so. The idea of him marking her turned her on.

Ian came back with a warm wet washcloth, shaking his head when she reached for it. "No, this is my job," he said, carefully cleaning his come from her body. He walked back to the bathroom and she heard him rinsing out the washcloth. He hadn't told her to move so she remained on the mat, wondering what would happen next. Was she supposed to get dressed now?

But then he came back with a fresh, wet cloth and sponged her body down, cleaning the drying arousal from her thighs and soothing her bottom. The washcloth rubbed across her nipples, reminding her of yesterday's adventure. Even though Ian was bringing their experience to an end for the evening, her nipples budded into tight peaks at his attention.

This was a different side to him, one she didn't get to see on the videos online. He was taking such good care of her, and so sweetly. It was a little hard to wrap her head around the fact that the same hands that spanked the hell out of her earlier were now gently caressing her.

She'd better leave before she started thinking stupid things, like this was more than whatever it was.

"So," he said, handing her back her work scrubs. "You remember what I said about how I'm not the dating type of guy?"

Grace didn't answer. Why? Why did he have to bring that up now, when she would have been so much happier just to go home and imagine? Maybe he thought it was important to not lead her on, but his words stung more than the spanking. She threw her scrubs into her tote bag and pulled out the jeans and top she'd brought with her to change into.

"I get it, Ian. It's fine. You don't want me to think you'll ever be my boyfriend again. You really don't need to remind me."

"Actually I was going to say that since we were both probably planning on going home to eat, we may as well…eat together. If you're hungry, that is."

Grace finished dressing and looked at him. What game was he playing? "No."

Ian laughed. "You're not hungry?"

"No, I am hungry. But we're either going on a date or

we're not. If we're just meeting here for sex stuff, fine, we're not dating. But if I'm sucking your cock one second and you're inviting me out to eat the next, that's a date. And since you don't do that, then…no."

She pressed her lips firmly together. Did those words actually just come out of her mouth? And she just said "sucking your cock" like it was no big deal, when even the thought of doing that—much less casually dropping the words into conversation—would have never happened just last week. Ian had broken something loose inside her that had been wound too tightly, something that had been long-repressed.

Who'd have thought she was that kind of girl? And into *that* sort of thing?

He looked confused for a moment, as if he were taking in everything she'd said.

"Okay," he said finally.

"Okay what?"

"Okay, it's a date." He held his arm out to her. "Will you please come with me someplace that serves pancakes at midnight?"

Grace raised her eyebrows in surprise. *Because if he's asking me out on a date, then everything changes.*

CHAPTER FIVE

Ian looked down at Grace, hoping she didn't leave him hanging with his arm held out like an old-fashioned escort.

"I like pancakes," she said warily, and looped her arm through his.

Her warm body next to his, fully clothed, felt good. But he couldn't remember the last time he'd been out on a date before—well, before Grace. Dating the women he worked with was out of the question, although he had slept with some of the single ones in the past. But they weren't interested in a relationship with him anymore than he was interested in a relationship with them.

He locked up the studio behind them, enjoying having her walking beside him to his car.

"Allow me," he said, opening the car door for her. He hadn't been out with her in years, but hopefully he could still remember how to treat a woman when she wasn't tied up. And not just any woman—Grace. What was it about her that made him change his "no dating" policy tonight, when she was the woman who made him start that policy in the first place?

Despite their history together, the Grace at his side was a different woman than the Grace he'd left behind, as much as he was a different man now than he'd been back then. Maybe that's why he felt nervous. In its own strange way, this was a first date.

I've got to start again at some point, right? He couldn't stay single forever or he'd end up one of those perennial bachelors like George Clooney, and that only sounded like a good plan for a decade or two. At some point that plan—that dying alone plan—would start to get real old, real fast.

In an ideal world, he'd get a job that he could talk about in polite company, meet a nice woman, get married, and have 1.5 kids and dog. It bothered him that he had to lie to his mother about how he paid the bills.

His mother thought he was actually putting his law degree to use, the degree she and his father had paid for when he was young and unappreciative. Passing the bar despite his relatively minimal amount of studying could only be attributed to his photographic memory, and not the grueling hours his fellow colleagues put in. Ian never told his family that he quit the firm after only a few years as a junior lawyer, despite the fat paycheck and his honest passion for law. He couldn't bear to let Mom down. She loved telling everyone about her son, the lawyer, who passed the bar on his first attempt.

He glanced over at Grace, who looked beautiful, her make-up slightly smudged, staring out the windshield as he drove. The seatbelt crossed her shoulder and over her breast, an everyday sort of restraint that no one but him would find sexy on a woman, he supposed.

Only as a Dom did he get his real needs met. His deeper, more intense needs. And he'd rather live in a small apartment and work for a few hours a day making BDSM videos than have a big house, fancy car, and work seventy-hour weeks only to come home to a wife who'd have a heart attack if she knew what he really wanted to do to her in bed. That was the life he'd envisioned himself having when he was with Grace in the past. A shy, prude vanilla wife who'd never fulfill his needs.

But those things he'd want to do to his future wife…all the sexual torments and delights he'd perfected over the years working as a Dom…they didn't fit into his mental picture of "wife". Could the woman that he hog-tied and whipped at night be the one he sat across the dinner table from, talking about how their days went? Could a woman who wanted to be a kinky sex-slave at bedtime be the one taking care of their child during the day? The two worlds seemed impossibly far apart, as far as he was concerned. Like a dream that could never come true.

And so he'd left Grace to seek out the other side, despite how much he cared for her, though neither lifestyle alone completed him.

They pulled up to the all-night diner, brightly lit both inside and out.

"Thanks for taking me out," Grace said as he opened the diner's shiny double doors for her. "I appreciate the gesture."

He was saved from responding when the hostess came to seat them.

"Do you want caffeine or no caffeine?" he asked, nodding over to the waitress.

"At midnight?" She scanned the menu. "Decaf for sure, with a short stack of pancakes. I need to get some sleep tonight."

"Decaf for me too, then, I guess," he told the waitress, and ordered eggs to go with his pancakes.

"Is this weird for you?" she asked, cutting her pancakes carefully when they arrived. Instead of pouring syrup on top, she poured it on the side of her plate and dipped each bite into it. He watched, fascinated by the way her mouth moved when she chewed and swallowed. The same mouth that was on his cock not too long ago.

Great. Don't get a hard-on here. Baseball baseball baseball. Okay.

She was looking at him expectantly, and he realized

he never answered her question.

"Am I acting like this is weird?" he asked, turning it back on her.

"You've told me numerous times that you're not the dating type, basically that we'll never be together again, and tonight you asked me on a date. Was it just because I coerced you into it, or did something change your mind?"

"I don't get coerced into doing things I don't want to do," he said, watching her eyes carefully for a reaction.

She smiled tentatively. "But I think you'd have a panic attack if I told you that these pancakes mean we're dating, am I right?"

Yes. No. Fuck.

"I don't have panic attacks," he said. "But I've missed you. And I've been thinking that I should probably change my policy on dating if a nice girl came along."

"Am I a nice girl?" Her lips hovered over a piece of pancake on her fork, as if she were waiting for him to respond before she'd take a bite.

"That's what I'm having a hard time figuring out," he admitted. "You're compassionate, obviously, or you wouldn't have been concerned about the other actresses' well-being. And you're a nurse, which is a good, respectable job—"

"Are you saying the women you work with at the website are somehow less respectable than me? Because that is such a double standard. What about you? You work there too."

"Maybe it is a double standard. But I'm not excluding myself. I have no illusions that what I do is something to write home about."

Grace put her fork down. She seemed upset and he had no idea why, since he'd been complimenting her. Where had he gone wrong?

"You need to respect all women," she said, "not just the women you deem worthy of your respect because they seem like "nice girls". I'm sure the actresses you work with are all nice girls, and you shouldn't blow them off as unworthy of dating just because of their job. It's your job too, after all." She stared into her coffee cup, gripping the handle until her knuckles turned white.

Ahh. So that's where she was going with this.

"You misunderstood me," he said quietly. "I most certainly *do* respect women who know what they want sexually, who aren't shy about their sexuality and their bodies, and who make an honest living, even if it's on a BDSM porn site. And I treat them with respect when we do scenes together."

"But they're not good enough to bring home to mom, is that it?" she asked. "And I'm…what's the word you used? Vanilla? You broke up with me because you think I'm so vanilla, I know you did. But now it makes me safe and okay to date, is that right?"

"You didn't seem so vanilla when you were over my knee, coming all over yourself while I spanked the hell out of you."

Her perfectly-shaped mouth dropped open and she gasped, quickly turning her head from side to side as if to see if anyone had overheard him, since he hadn't exactly kept his voice down. No one was looking at them.

A pretty pink blush crept up her cheeks. "I don't know what I am, Ian. I really don't. If you'd asked me three years ago to bend over I'd have probably not been into it. It wasn't until I saw…those videos…that I realized how hot it could be. I've never done that sort of thing before."

"And I've never done this sort of thing before," he admitted, gesturing at the two of them sitting, eating a meal together. On a date with a woman he cared for who also knew his true predilections in bed.

"Then I guess we're both on new territory," she whispered.

"So maybe I should learn how to play the boyfriend again for you, and you could learn how to be my after-hours sex-slave for me."

"No, you've got it backward, Ian," she said, smiling. "If you're going to learn how to play the boyfriend, as you put it—it wouldn't be for my sake. It would be for your own."

He laughed. She was right. He needed to get over his fear of dating, especially now that he'd reconnected with the one girl he'd never forgiven himself for leaving. Grace wasn't afraid to tell him what he needed to be told, even if it upset him. It was an unusual trait for a submissive, which was probably why he wasn't used to it.

Grace wasn't a submissive. But she wasn't vanilla, either. And she didn't seem to like being referred to as a "nice girl" in a way that differentiated her from the "nice girls" that he tied up and whipped on the website.

"Perhaps that's true," he admitted. "And perhaps if you want to learn how to be my sex-slave, it would be for your own benefit."

Grace smiled and took a sip of her coffee. "Oh, I already knew that it would be for me. Why do you think I came to you in the first place?"

*****

Later that night, Grace couldn't fall asleep, even though she'd only drunk the decaf coffee. The conversation she'd had with Ian kept replaying itself in her mind. Well, the conversation, and the other stuff. The spanking. The blowjob. The mind-boggling orgasm he gave her.

But out of all of the evening's experiences, what she couldn't figure out was—why date her again now, after so long? She'd certainly seemed to surprise him by being open to kinky stuff. It didn't seem right that Ian thought she was somehow more "dateable" than all of the other women he'd played with over the years. If she'd agreed to be on the website for the whole world to see, would he have immediately relegated her to the un-dateable category and waited for some other "nice" girl to come into his life?

It didn't make sense. He had her as when she truly was young and innocent, and apparently he couldn't stand the idea of never being able to express his true sexual desires.

And now that he had told her his true needs…could she be that for him? Could she be both?

She didn't want to be just the nice girl anymore. How could she know if Ian was really interested in dating her again, or just in the idea of dating someone he'd always thought of as "respectable" now that he was reevaluating his long-term relationship goals? She needed to be with someone who respected her as a person, not just her job or so-called vanilla lifestyle. How ironic, that he was drawn to her for being vanilla but relished when she let herself be seduced by his dominance.

As she drifted off to sleep, the answer came to her.

She would be herself around him—nice, naughty, respectable, slut, whatever she felt like being—and let him introduce her to experiences she'd never thought she'd ever wanted before she first saw him on the website. The man who held the whip… But she still had a point to prove, and there was only one way to find out how Ian truly felt about her.

At some point in the near future, she'd just have to star in one of the BDSM porn website's videos after all…

CHAPTER SIX

Grace received a text message from Ian the following afternoon while she was at work.

Grace, I'd love either a repeat of the meal we shared or what came before it. You?

She laughed as she quickly replied:

I vote for both, but perhaps in a more traditional order. Or have you forgotten you're supposed to feed a girl *before* you attempt to get in her pants?

Ian's response was typed clumsily. *Pick u up ur house 8pm? Text me ur address.*

Grace imagined he was on the set, and they were calling him to get moving. Ugh. The thought of him tying up and touching another woman, especially after what they shared last night…it just didn't sit well with her. Then again, she'd had to live with the idea of Ian being with another woman the whole time they'd been separated. Their tentative reunion—she barely had him comfortable with the idea of dating her, much less dating exclusively, much less quitting his job over her. So.

She re-read what Ian wrote and sighed. He was obviously in a rush now.

Have a nice shoot, she replied, adding a frowny face emoticon and then deleting it.

*****

Ian knocked on her apartment door only a few minutes past eight. He would have been on time but he

71

had to sit in his Jeep for a few minutes blasting heavy metal to psych himself up first. Then he was psyched but nervous, so he played a low-key country song from an AM station until his nerves stopped jangling, and headed up the elevator to Grace's apartment with an old Tim McGraw song stuck in his head.

Why be nervous? It wasn't like he hadn't already walked this path to her apartment before, many times when they used to date. But being on a date with her last night was like dating a whole new woman. A woman who'd been an enticing combination of the girl he'd once loved and left…and a woman who might now be open to the idea of him being dominant in the bedroom. Hell, she'd already blown him…and done it exquisitely, despite her earlier protestations that she'd be no good at it.

He checked his watch at the same time her door swung open.

"Hi," "Hello," they both said simultaneously.

She wore a red sundress with matching red lipstick. It was both girly and so fucking sexy he wanted to claim her right then, just push into her apartment and fuck her right there on the floor.

"You look beautiful," he said, eliciting a shy smile. A shy smile on red-painted lips. He had to take a deep breath to remind himself now wasn't sex time. It was date time.

"So do you," she replied, and then blushed, laughing like she always seemed to do when she was nervous. "I mean…never mind. Let's go."

He took her hand, never crossing the threshold to her apartment, and gave a little tug until she fell into his arms. Grace looked up at him with a surprised gasp.

It took all of his concentration to not kiss her, considering how close her lips were to his…those bright, lipstick-red lips. Oh God.

And then she stood on her tippy toes and kissed him, surprising him more than he could ever have done to her. No, Grace was no submissive. And that didn't bother him in the slightest. Had he assumed all this time that he'd need someone in the lifestyle, a permanent slave?

Yes. His bedroom predilections for kink and everything he'd seen on his favorite BDSM forums online all pointed toward finding a partner for the Dominant/submissive life...someone to cherish and collar and own.

But Grace would never be owned by anyone, he could see that. She was her own woman, but she had a kinky streak a mile long, he could tell. She wasn't vanilla, but she wasn't a sub. Grace would find herself a regular vanilla husband, no doubt.

"But you'd miss the sex," he muttered against her lips, scarcely aware he'd spoken the words aloud and not just in his head.

"I'd miss what sex?"

Fuck. He laughed. "You caught me so off-guard with that kiss that now I'm talking to myself." He laughed again and leaned in to kiss her again, deeply, hoping she'd forget her line of questioning.

"You said, 'but you'd miss the sex,'" she said. "As far as I recall, you were never interested in our sex life when we dated before, so there wouldn't be much to miss."

"I'm sorry you felt that way." Ian forced himself to hold eye-contact, to not glance away in discomfort. "I think it was because I hid my true sexual predilections from you."

"I know," she whispered. "That must've made it hard for you to connect with me during sex."

"Well, now that you know the real me, we should remedy that."

A lascivious grin played across her beautiful face. "Perhaps we should. But I demand a proper date first."

Demand? He stifled his laughter at her word choice. The girl had no idea that the women he usually found sexy never spoke to him like that...so why did he find her so damn desirable?

"And I intend to be a good date," he said. He didn't want to make her less feisty, or turn her into a something she wasn't. Hell, it was fun talking to someone who wasn't afraid of him, and who didn't back down.

It would be even more fun to spank her for it later...when it was time.

They walked hand in hand down to his Jeep, and he gave her a boost to get in, enjoying the chance to put his hands on her bottom. She swatted him playfully.

"Watch those hands—I'm still sore! Where are we going for dinner?" she asked. Not a question a submissive would ask.

"I was thinking Chinese, is that okay?" And that wasn't something a Dom would say. But it was so easy to talk to her without any roles or games or power play when they were out and about like this. Could he live a life like this?

As long as I get my kink on at night, yes. The realization felt good, like the date with Grace had suddenly become very important.

"I love Chinese!" she replied, and sat back in her seat, looking out the window, the seatbelt strap binding her beautifully.

Grace fit with him so perfectly, somehow. With her, he had immediately felt at home, from the moment he first saw her standing in front of the studio's door.

Over lo mein and pork fried rice, she brought it up again. "So what did you mean then, that I would miss the sex?"

"You're not a submissive. Someday, you'll marry some vanilla guy and you'll probably be very happy...but you'll miss the sex. That's what was running through my head when I said that." Better to be honest from the start.

"You're right," she agreed, rolling the noodles with her fork and forsaking the chopsticks. "I'm no submissive, and I have no desire to be one. But..." she dropped her voice to a whisper and leaned in. "It gets me so hot when you tell me what to do when we were playing. I like the playing."

"And I like playing with you too." He smiled. Man, that was the understatement of the year.

"But this—" she gestured between them, indicating their low-key date. "Do you like this too?"

She looked cute, her brow furrowed with concern. Here he was worrying he'd scare her off in the bedroom and she was worried she'd scare him with the non-BDSM day-to-day stuff.

"I love it," he admitted. "I feel very comfortable with you."

"Me too." She paused, a mischievous smile playing on those red lips. "Do you need a safeword, in case things get too normal for you, and you need me to stop being vanilla for a moment and I don't know, kneel or something?"

Ian laughed so hard he sputtered ice water from his cup. "Check, please!" he called. "I think we need to have enough sex that you'll know what you'll be missing, what do you think?"

"Absolutely."

*****

"I can't believe you brought an overnight bag." Grace laughed as they walked down the hallway to her apartment.

"I know. Very presumptuous of me," he winked. "But I figured you wouldn't have the sorts of toys I like to play with."

Toys? Images from the videos he'd done for the website flashed through her mind. Whatever was in Ian's backpack couldn't be too crazy, right? After all, it had to fit in the backpack.

Grace's hand shook as she turned the key and unlocked her apartment door. She'd barely gotten the door open and shut again before Ian dropped his bag on the floor and pushed her up against the wall, pinning her arms above her head.

"Hi," she said, looking him straight in the eye with a

smile she hoped covered her nerves. At least she wasn't blushing. Trembling all over, yes, but not blushing. Thank God.

"Not the response I was looking for," he said, pressing in close to her. "Now that I have you, what shall I do with you?"

"Anything you want, Sir."

His kiss came hard and fast, devouring her lips, her mouth, nipping at her neck. "Good girl."

"I'm not such a good girl if I'm here with you, now am I, Sir?" she teased, and squealed as he hoisted her over his shoulder, fireman-style. Her dress flew up, exposing her panties. A cool breeze from the air-conditioning vent caressed her bare thighs.

"Bedroom. Now," he demanded, smacking her ass through the light material of her panties.

"Second door to the left," she replied breathlessly, forgetting that he knew exactly where her bedroom door was. This new Ian was so different when it was time for sex. And she liked it.

He spanked her again, striding down the hallway so fast the carpet beneath his feet seemed to blur, at least to her upside-down vantage point.

Grace shrieked, laughing, when he tossed her on the middle of her queen-sized bed.

He stared her down. "You laugh when you're nervous. Are you nervous now, Grace?"

"I was, then I wasn't," she answered. "Now I am again. You look…intense."

"Do you remember your safeword?"

Yes, because I picked "safeword" as my safeword, like a newbie moron, she thought, but aloud she only said "Yes, Sir."

"Take off your clothes."

She sat up, grateful to not have any buttons or zippers to mess with. Her sundress lifted easily over her head and she tossed it on the floor, something she'd never normally do. The carpet in her bedroom was spotless, all of her clothes either in the hamper or neatly hung in the closet. But being with Ian made her feel an urgency she'd never felt with any other lover before…including the Ian she remembered from their past relationship. Sex with Ian without any secrets between them was clearly a whole new ballgame.

"You're so beautiful," he said, pulling off his own T-shirt. His chiseled abs looked spectacular in the shadows thrown off by her bedside lamp. "Let me help you with that bra."

Kneeling on the bed, he wrapped his arms around her and expertly dispatched her brassiere. God he smelled good. Not like cologne, or aftershave. It was subtler than that. Maybe she was smelling his deodorant. Either way, she wanted to nuzzle her face against his skin and inhale him.

"Do you want to see what's in my backpack?" he asked.

She'd almost forgotten about his overnight bag. Had he even brought it into her room?

"Silence implies consent," he said, pulling the bag up onto her bed.

"What if I said no?" she asked, not because she wanted to say no, but because the idea that silence implied consent sounded very much like a rule she needed to remember.

"Then that's also consent."

"What?" she couldn't take her eyes off his bag, and how he unzipped it ceremoniously.

"You can say no all you want. I won't stop unless you safeword, or if I decide to stop." He paused, reached out and held her chin in his large hand. "Do not forget that. *No* and *stop* are not your safewords. Silence is not your safeword. I have no intention of taking you to a point where you feel the need to stop me for real, but if you do that's the way to do it. Do you understand?"

"Yes, Sir." She felt safe with him, with his straightforwardness. What was he going to pull out of that bag?

Handcuffs. Two pairs. Two? Why two? But he seemed so very in control right then, so dominant, that she didn't feel right questioning him. Maybe later, when they were done playing, and back to being...just them. Whatever they were.

Dating. A couple. Lovers. Master/slave. What are we?

"Lie back, Grace, hands at your sides."

She obeyed, feeling very naked and vulnerable, though he still hadn't removed her panties. They were damp now with her desire for him, for what he offered her. Freedom to let someone else take charge. She didn't have to worry about anything, it was all in his hands. And from what she remembered, his hands were more than capable...

"Knees up, spread your legs."

Her hip cracked as she shifted into the unfamiliar position. Stopping her Pilates lessons had been a mistake. Ian snapped a cuff onto her right wrist, and she gasped at the feel of metal encircling her wrist.

Cold, hard steel. Ian's finger slipped under the cuff, right by her radial pulse, and she smiled, appreciating the fact that he was checking to make sure the handcuff wasn't so tight it would impair her circulation. He would have been a good RN, if hadn't picked "professional Dom" as his career choice. Even with his sexually sadistic streak, he was so caring and thoughtful.

Ian pushed her thighs apart wider, holding her right ankle next to her cuffed right wrist, and suddenly she knew exactly why he needed two pairs of handcuffs for one woman.

He cuffed her wrist and ankle together, and made quick work of cuffing her wrist to her ankle on the other side as well, checking her circulation with impressive skill.

"Now there's nowhere to go," Ian said, smiling down at her.

Nowhere to go. The thought appealed. There was no

other place she'd rather be than handcuffed with her legs spread wide under Ian. He pulled his jeans off, and his boxer-briefs.

He stretched over her body like a large panther, letting her feel some of his weight as he put his lips to her ear. A trickle of his pre-come dripped onto her inner thigh.

"Are you okay?" he whispered.

"Yes, Sir," she whispered back, turning her mouth toward his. "I'm exactly where I want to be."

"I have another toy for you."

She tried to raise her head to see what he was getting out of the bag, but it was useless. *Nowhere to go.* She'd just have to wait until he showed her. Lying back, a familiar sense of comfort flowed through her, followed by the less familiar spike of desire. Only Ian made her pant with need like this, with anticipation.

They hadn't even had his new brand of sex yet, and she already knew she'd miss it.

What if I don't have to miss it? What if...

No sense in thinking about their future right now. Now was for the present, and the toy in an unopened package that Ian held above her face for her to see.

"Oh my God," she said, laughing, her stupid nervous laugh that gave her away every time, to Ian least.

"Have you ever seen a butt plug, Grace?"

"Y-yes." She'd stopped laughing. The website had a clip of a girl slowly sitting on a huge plug attached to a chair. Nothing had ever gone in her asshole before, although she knew the area was filled with sensitive nerve endings.

Ian closed her legs, manipulating her whole body like a marionette. Lifting her half off the bed by her ankles, he slapped the backs of her thighs and her ass, which was still covered in her panties.

How was he going to get her panties off with her ankles in cuffs?

"Yes what?" he prompted.

What? Oh shit. She'd forgotten already. "Yes, *Sir*. I've seen one before, on the website."

"I bought this just for you, Grace. Don't worry, it's small and it won't get lost inside you, not with the flared base."

Incredible how he'd read her mind, her fears, and allayed them so quickly. How did he do that?

"I'm going to lube you up, and put this in, and then I'm going to finally get a taste of that delicious pussy of yours."

He pressed his face against her panties, inhaling her scent. She was so wet she could smell her own arousal. If Ian hadn't seemed so turned-on by it, she'd be embarrassed. Instead, she could see Ian's cock had been hard this entire time. His desire for her made her feel womanly and sensual and cherished, even as he talked about taboo things like putting toys in her ass.

He rubbed his hands over her hips, caressing her.

"This might hurt," he warned.

Oh my God. What was going to hurt? She froze, not breathing, not daring to move a muscle.

"Sometimes," he murmured, running his finger across the top on her cotton panties, tickling her sensitive skin, "I like it rough." With a primal grunt, he ripped her underwear off her body with a ferocity that left her breathless.

She whimpered, suddenly terrified and aroused at the same time. Her skin stung where the elastic had snapped against it, where he'd torn her panties from her hips.

"I'll be gentle now," he said, sliding his fingers along her wet slit.

"Don't be."

He licked his fingers, shiny with her arousal, one by one. "I'm going to eat you for a very long time. And you're going to lie there and let me, now aren't you?"

"I don't believe I have much of a choice," she lied, pulling on the metal handcuffs just to feel them bite into her skin. He was right, playing was so much fun. Every dirty fantasy she'd ever had could be indulged with Ian, guilt-free, because he allowed her to pretend it was all his doing, all his fault. And she was just the unfortunate woman who happened to be cuffed on a bed by such a merciless, gorgeous man. She grinned, and he flicked her clit with his fingers.

"Ow!" she gasped.

"This might hurt a bit too," he said, rubbing lubricant over the length of the butt plug, "but I think you like a little pain. You're dripping all over the bed."

Heat rose up from her breasts to her cheeks, because he was right.

The tip of the plug pressed against her asshole, and she tensed automatically.

"Breathe," he told her. "Let me in."

She cried out as he pushed the plug past her anal sphincter, filling her.

"Good girl," he said, and she paused, feeling the alien sensation of having an object inside of her. Her asshole felt like it was on fire.

Ian spread her knees farther apart and settled himself between her legs, holding her thighs open with his large hands. He lapped at her juices, sucking her clit into his mouth.

Oh my. The pleasure mingled with the pain he'd just given her, entwined together in an exquisite feeling unlike anything she'd experienced before.

She closed her eyes and relaxed, enjoying herself during oral sex for the first time in her life. With her previous lovers, she felt like it was a bargaining chip that men used to exchange for sexual favors from her. She certainly couldn't climax from their half-hearted attempts, drawing the alphabet on her clitoris with their tongues, if they could find her clit at all.

But knowing that Ian had been fantasizing about having her tied up and being able to eat her out for as long as he wanted…well, that made her—

"Oh, my God, don't stop," she moaned, her climax peaking.

"Stop?" Ian laughed, his words vibrating against her pussy. "I haven't even started."

He ignored her cries of protest as he continued licking her, sucking her, through her first orgasm and finally past a third—at which point she was breathless from coming so hard, so many times, with no break.

"Please," she begged. "Fuck me. Fuck me, I need you inside me."

She heard the rip of foil and the flutter of the condom wrapper, and then he held himself over her, staring into her eyes.

"Oh, I'll fuck you alright."

With that, he thrust himself deep inside her, filling her pussy completely. With the plug still in her ass, her inner muscles clamped tightly around him, milking his cock. His thickness touched every nerve ending inside, simultaneously hitting her g-spot and some other spots that should probably also be named if they weren't already. The force of his cock gliding in and out of her promised to deliver an earth-shattering climax.

The handcuffs restrained her from raking her fingernails down his back the way she wanted to, to give him a taste of the exquisite pleasure-pain he inflicted upon her with each pounding thrust.

Her scent lingered on his mouth and he kissed her with a primal fierceness that matched his fucking. She licked his lips, tasting herself.

He pulled the plug out of her ass, and she screamed and came so hard she nearly bucked him off of her, but he held tight and rode her through her climax. Her head snapped forward with the intensity of the sensation.

"Fuck me, fuck me, please Sir, fuck me," she gasped, scarcely aware she was speaking at all. Everything was sensation, and pleasure, and pain, and Ian. Especially Ian.

When he finally came inside her, she felt his cock pulsate as the force of his come hit the condom. He collapsed on top of her, pressing his lips to the pounding carotid pulse in her neck.

"I don't want to have to miss the sex," she whispered.

"And I don't want to miss you."

Tomorrow. Tomorrow she'd find out if she could integrate her life with Ian's world, and vice versa. If he still wanted to be with her after she'd shed any pretense of being vanilla or a "nice" girl...

The conundrum circled through her mind. He'd dated her three years ago when she was the vanilla nice girl, but broke up with her because his sexual needs weren't met. Now that his needs were being met as a Dom, he wouldn't date the girls he played with because they didn't fit his definition of a "good girl," even if he protested that fact. Quite simply, he hadn't dated anyone since he'd left her, and he'd had plenty of subs to choose from.

Would he still respect her as an equal if she was submissive to him in the bedroom? His muscular arms around her felt so right. Like home. She didn't want to have to miss him either.

CHAPTER SEVEN

Grace used a vacation day so she could drive over to the studio during regular shooting hours. If she didn't use her allotted vacation days, she'd lose them, after all, just like she lost them last year. It amounted to her working for her asshole of a doctor for free. That and the anticipation of what lay ahead kept her from feeling too much guilt over playing hooky from the doctor's office.

She entered the unlocked door without knocking, closing it quietly behind her. From the looks of the activity on the set, they were setting up a shot with Nikki and filming all of the set-up as part of the new video.

Ian probably wouldn't even notice she walked in, since she'd been so discreet about it. Still, a pang of jealousy hit her as she saw him working.

Ian laughed and flirted with Nikki as he walked around her naked body, securing her ankles and wrists to the spanking bench. She smiled back at him, wiggling her ass as if to tease him.

Grace stifled the impulse to roll her eyes. But at least she knew Ian playing the role of Dom to Nikki didn't mean he wanted to be with Nikki, not like how he seemed to want to be with Grace. Although it wasn't as if they were an official couple. Or were they—could they ever be?

Only one way to find out.

And now she had front row seats to watch Ricardo's crew video-taping Ian as he dripped hot candle wax in very pretty splatters all over Nikki's back. She arched her back as the drops of wax hit her skin, as if to try and get away from the sensation even though she was tied up and at Ian's mercy.

At Ian's mercy. God, why did Grace want that too? She should be getting upset watching him play with another woman, and instead Grace found herself getting more and more aroused. She could imagine what it would feel like to have the drips of hot wax fall on her skin and to be forced to endure it, and she knew if it were her tied to that bench instead of Nikki, she'd be so wet her desire would be evident even on video.

Watching Ian work was different from watching the porn downloads at home, because this time, she could focus on him and not the girl. How his brow furrowed with concentration as he planned and executed each erotic movement. How his eyes lit up with desire when the submissive bound before him moaned in pleasure-pain.

Did he want to be dominant in every aspect of a relationship? Grace didn't think so, because he'd specifically told her that he was called Sir during a scene, and in the bedroom. To her that meant outside the bedroom he could be just Ian.

And did Grace want to date "just Ian" again? As in, be with him when he was her equal, a man she dated—not the man pinching her nipples or spanking her?

Absolutely, but she supposed she'd need more dates with him to find out if they could keep up this new arrangement of vanilla by day, kinky by night. Would he even want to go out with her again if she became just another actress on the porn site?

Maybe she should keep herself separate from his job. Shouldn't show up on the set anymore, not even after hours. They could meet somewhere else.

But then she'd never know if he was only dating her for her comparative innocence. And innocent girls didn't star in porn websites. If only he'd been open with her in the past, instead of leaving her...

But then I would have probably freaked out and left him. I wasn't ready back then.

"Ahh, look who's here," Ricardo said, catching her eye.

Grace nodded politely, not wanting to interrupt the scene Ian and Nikki were doing, but apparently the audio was poor enough that if Ricardo spoke to her on the other side of the set it wouldn't have too much of an effect on the taping.

"I thought you were scared off for good," he said.

"I...I was. I figured I'd come watch a shoot before deciding if it's something I could do," she replied. It was sort of true.

"Give it a shot, if you don't like it you can use your safeword, no harm no foul," Ricardo urged.

Tempting. Very tempting. But it wasn't the fear of having to use her safeword that kept her from jumping at the offer. What if Ian never wanted to date her again if she became—officially—one of the...not-so-nice girls?

That's why she had to do. She didn't want to date a man who wouldn't be with her just for doing the same exact thing he was doing. It was a double standard she couldn't allow to stand.

"Okay, I'm in."

"Wonderful," Ricardo said. "I'll get the contract."

Ian walked over after he'd finished his shoot with Nikki. Nikki was smoking topless in the corner with a very satisfied smile playing on her lips.

"Hey, Grace," Ian said, giving her a kiss on the cheek. "A visit at work? What a pleasant surprise."

The kiss threw her mentally for a moment. Did he always kiss women he knew on the cheek in greeting? Or was that just for her, now that they were dating? He didn't sound upset that she was on the set, just surprised.

Ricardo came back with the paperwork. "Ian, you remember our nineteen-year-old virgin, Grace, right? She's here to work. What do you want to do with her?"

The smile fell off of Ian's handsome face and he turned to Grace. "I thought we agreed this wasn't the place for you. That you don't want to be on the internet on a porn website forever."

Ricardo huffed. "So it was you who scared her off? Not cool, man, not cool."

Ian ignored his boss and spoke to her as if she were the only person in the room, although at this point it was clear that everyone had stopped what they were doing so they could listen to the argument.

Grace's pulse pounded in her ears. "I'm here because I want to know why you won't date girls you work with. And if I do a video, I want to know if I'll be deemed unacceptable as girlfriend material. Because if that's the case, I don't even need to do the shoot. I can just leave right now, and never see you again."

Please, Ian, please prove to me how you really feel.

*****

Ian forced himself to exhale slowly, to stay calm. Grace just didn't get it. He didn't have a double standard—at least, not anymore. After Grace took him to task for his thinking he realized he had to reanalyze everything. He'd never spent too much time thinking about it before, it was just one of those things. Girls who he tied up at work were sexy but not girlfriends, girls who he dated were nice but not sexy...or at least, not his personal type of sexy. That had been the reason he'd left her before.

But now he knew it was possible for the women he worked with to be more than just porn actresses. They could be in a relationship as well, because that's what he wanted—to have his kink and have a life outside of it. But he couldn't see any of the women he worked with as the sort of woman he could be in a real relationship with, because they weren't...they weren't Grace. Something about her was a game-changer, and he couldn't put his finger on what it was.

"It's not that you'd be unacceptable as girlfriend material, Grace."

"Well?" she asked, staring up at him defiantly, making it clear for all to see that she was not submissive in the slightest outside of the bedroom. Or dungeon. "What is it then?"

"You're a nurse. You're not going to be happy with yourself a month from now, a year from now, whenever, if you do this."

"So you'd still date me if I did a video with you?" she asked, challenging him.

Before he'd reunited with her, he'd have said no, because in his previous way of thinking, if a girl did a porn video then she wasn't going to be interested in doing anything else, any normal stuff, like eating pancakes at midnight.

But Grace was a woman he could have fun with both inside and outside of the bedroom. It didn't matter if she was newly discovering her sexuality, and choosing to do it in a public manner, at that. All that mattered was making sure he still got to be with her. He couldn't lose the one girl he'd found who made his dreams seem like a real possibility, instead of just a dream. Dreams of getting married to a woman he could tie up and spank, but also go to the movies, on vacations, and even to the playground with their kids. Yeah, he could see Grace doing all those things. With him.

"I'd still date you no matter what you did," Ian replied.

Grace smiled up at him. "Really? So you really thought about what I said at the pancake house, huh."

"You could say that," he laughed, and in front of everyone, he put his arm around her waist, pulled her in close, and kissed her. She tasted like strawberry lip-gloss and something else uniquely Grace-scented.

Ricardo coughed. "Now that we've all kissed and

made up, are we shooting a video or what?"

"Yes," Ian replied. "But only if you don't show her face."

"No deal," Ricardo said. "Our subscribers love seeing the girls faces when they scream and when they come, you know that."

Nikki stood up from the corner, stubbing out her cigarette. "I have an idea," she said.

*****

Grace looked over at her, surprised. Not nearly as surprised as she was by the fact that Ian was willing to date her even if she was in the porn video. And she did sort of like the idea of not showing her face, since then she'd never have to worry about someone being positive they'd seen her.

Nikki walked over. "You blindfold her with a big blindfold that covers half her face, and put one of the wigs on her. If Master Ian here can manage to not gag her for the shoot, she'll have plenty of facial expressions with just her mouth and no one will know it's her."

Ricardo cocked his head to the side as if he were envisioning it. "Yeah. That could work. Get me a wig."

Wow. This is really happening.

Nikki brought out a short blonde wig with bangs, and helped her tuck her long hair underneath it and pin it in place. Since everyone was used to seeing Grace as a brunette, the change was impressive. With her fair skin, she was certainly passable as a blonde, especially since the wig's bangs in the front were long enough to cover her dark eyebrows.

Ricardo walked them over to the dark leather spanking bench, adjusting a light in a way that made no obvious difference to her, but that elicited a thumbs up from the large, handsome man looking through the viewfinder on the camera.

Ian turned to that crew member behind the tripod. "We need to film this a bit differently. "I'm going to be facing the camera, she'll be dressed and facing me. I'll blindfold her, and once her identity is properly hidden, you can shoot how you like."

Ricardo nodded to the crew and clapped his hands. "Let's do this, we're wasting time!"

Ian stood just like he said, looking right at her but facing the camera so her back was to them. It made her feel a little more at ease to only have to look at Ian, and not at the lights and the other men watching...

Am I really doing this? Am I going to wake up soon or is this real?

She laughed nervously, and Ian smiled.

"You're so distracted, honey," he said, effectively nicknaming her despite the fact that she'd completely forgotten she'd need a fake name to go with her new look. "I'm going to blindfold you so all you can focus on is me, and the experience I give you."

"Yes, Sir," she said, hoping the mike would pick it up. Just in case it didn't, she nodded her head vigorously.

He carefully tied the blindfold on over the wig and over her eyes, his hands so warm as they brushed against her face. The material was thin enough she could still see vague shadows from underneath it. Would this hide her identity? Did it matter?

But she liked that Ian was being so protective of her. And that he wanted to do this with her without letting it affect their outside relationship.

"I'm going to take all of your clothes off. Be cooperative, honey, like a good girl."

He turned her around, and she imagined that now she was facing the cameras. So many men were watching her...and Nikki, too, probably, smoking her cigarettes in the corner perhaps.

A shiver of desire ran through her. Perhaps she did have an exhibitionist streak in her after all. Ian pulled her tank top up from the bottom, past her bra and over her arms. With her arms lifted in the air, Ian took both of her wrists in one of his large hands and ran his other hand over the curves of her body, slowly undoing the clasp on her bra and removing it, letting it fall to the floor.

Cool air hit her nipples, and they beaded into tight peaks. It wasn't just the cold, though, that did it. It was Ian, and his hard cock pressed against her ass as he stood behind her, undressing her for the world to see.

He let go of her wrists and unzipped her shorts, sliding them down her thighs, taking the time to caress her legs as he pulled them off of her. Only her panties remained.

Thank God I'm blindfolded. I can't imagine watching the entire crew watching me.

Actually, yes, she could, and her panties dampened at the thought.

Ian pulled her panties off and pressed them softly by her face until she nuzzled into them, inhaling her own musk like she knew he wanted her to do, just as he had wanted her to lick his fingers that night after he'd played with her pussy.

"Your scent is so sexy," he murmured in her ear, and she smiled. "Now, I'm going to lean you over this bench and restrain you, honey."

"Yes, Sir." But what would he do after that? The possibilities were endless, and the anticipation was almost unbearable.

"Patience," he said, and from the heat in her cheeks she knew she was blushing. It was if he could read her mind.

Ian took control of her body, guiding her as if in a dance until she was positioned exactly the way he wanted her to be over the bench, facing away from the main camera.

"When you first came here," he said, lightly spanking her ass, waking up her nerve endings, "you said that I was the one who held the whip." He spanked her some more, warming her up, and she could barely concentrate on his words because with the blindfold on she was completely in-tune to the sensations on her skin. The heat. The sting. His hand, caressing her ass before smacking it again.

"I'm going to whip you now, for the first time, is that correct?"

"Yes, Sir."

"Do you remember your safeword?"

"Yes, Sir." Her body shook with adrenaline. *Please*, she thought, but she didn't know what she was hoping for, what she wanted.

More. Yes. She wanted more of whatever Ian wanted to give her.

She gasped as a thick leather rope glided over her skin. He was showing her what the whip looked like as if she were a blind woman, it seemed. She could envision it now, and imagined it was long and black like so many of the instruments of pleasure-pain the dungeon had to offer. The tail slid over her back slowly, as if to give her a feel for the length and weight of the whip.

If her legs weren't tied apart, she'd squirm just so she could feel her clit move against her own flesh. But in this open position, her movement only succeeded in rubbing her clit against the bench a bit, not nearly enough. She moaned.

"My dear, we haven't even begun," Ian said, and with that, the first lash hit.

It felt like a static shock, the kind you get after shuffling across the carpet and then touching a metal doorknob, except this shock was long, lining her back from one shoulder to her opposite hip. She took in a sharp breath of air, barely getting a sound out before the whip came down again.

"You're so beautiful," Ian said, and whipped her again, and again, until her entire world shrunk down to include only her, and Ian, and the whip.

The whip, the whip, the whip...

She rubbed her clit against the bench, moving her

hips in time to the lashes, and suddenly she heard the whip drop with a thud to the rubber-matted floor and Ian's hands grasped her around the waist.

"Please, Sir," she whispered, and he complied, reaching around so his long fingers were between her and the bench. He rubbed her clit hard and fast, her juices making her so slippery that she could feel him pausing to wipe them across her naked thighs so he could get more friction.

Had he done this to any of the other girls on the videos? She didn't think he had. He'd always used a vibrator, something between him and the girls. But with her, he seemed to have no problem getting physical.

Oh my God, is he going to fuck me in front of everyone?

The thought excited her, but it wasn't going to happen. It just wasn't that sort of site. It was all about the BDSM, and the pain, and the pleasure...the pleasure...she gasped as Ian rubbed harder, faster, pinching her clit.

She screamed and bucked her hips, pulling against all four restraints as she climaxed. Through the blindfold she could see a man with a camera focused on her face as Ian tortured her by slowing down but not stopping once she came.

"Please, please," she gasped. "I came." *You can stop now.* But she wouldn't safeword. Not for a little over-stimulation.

"You have a choice, honey," Ian said, his voice thick with desire, the same voice she'd heard whispering to her late at night after they'd made love. But this time it was meant to be shared...with her, with the other men in the room, and with everyone who would ever watch this video of her in bondage.

She moaned, wriggling her hips under his hand.

"Either you get twenty minutes of forced orgasms with my vibrator right on your virgin little nub, or you get a spanking—"

"Spanking, Sir!" she interrupted, practically shouting

it.

"Okay, but you didn't let me finish what I was saying." Removing his fingers from her clit, he was gone suddenly, and then seemed to appear out of nowhere directly in front of her, standing on the mat next to her face.

His fingers smelled like her arousal, and she blushed when he pressed them against her lips. Without him asking her to, she sucked them into her mouth. This time, it was Ian who groaned with desire. She smiled around his fingers, loving the fact that she turned him on as much as he turned her on.

"I'm going to spank your pussy," he said. "Aren't you sorry you interrupted me now?" He chuckled.

But no, she wasn't sorry. After an orgasm her clitoris was always so sensitized she couldn't handle having a buzzing vibrator pressed against it, not if it was anything like what she'd seen Ian do in those downloads. Images of him tying long white vibrators to the girls' thighs as they came over and over until they screamed flashed through her mind.

Ian was gone again, but then she felt his heat behind her. She had no idea where the camera was, what angle they were filming, and she didn't care. Half a dozen men and at least one other woman were watching her right now, and all she could focus on was Ian, and what he had in store for her.

Would it hurt?

"Are you ready, honey?" he asked.

"No, Sir." Grace would never be ready, but she wasn't safewording. She could do this.

"Then I'll give you a countdown. On three, honey. Breathe."

"Yes, Sir." Her whole body trembled with anticipation and adrenaline.

"One....Two...*Three*," he said, slapping his hand up between her thighs on the word "three"—directly on her clit.

She yelped, shocked by the sting of it, how it mingled with that specific intense pleasure that only her clitoris seemed capable of creating within her.

He spanked her pussy again, and she tried to slam her legs shut, forgetting until the restraints reminded her that she couldn't close her thighs.

"May I?" he asked, and this time she knew exactly what he meant.

"Yes, Sir."

His long finger slid inside her. "You're so wet, honey. Tell me you love when I spank your naughty pussy."

"I-I love it, Sir."

"Come for me," he whispered, and ground his palm against her clit, holding her captive with his cupped hand.

She couldn't help but to obey.

CHAPTER EIGHT

Ian waited until the cameras were off before he took off Grace's blindfold and untied her, carefully checking her fingers and toes for circulation, inspecting her ankles and wrists for ligature marks. The restraints had left her unharmed, the whip, however, had left its own special brand of light red welts across her beautiful pale back.

"Those will fade in a day or two," he said, as he helped her up. She stumbled into a hug, surprising him with her easy display of affection.

Ian wrapped his arms around her. "You're trembling. Are you okay?"

She smiled up at him, pulling the hair pins off the blonde wig, and let her beautiful long brunette hair loose. "Better than okay. That was probably the most adventurous thing I've ever done in my life."

"That scene felt so different to me," he admitted. "It wasn't like when I usually work."

"Oh no, was I that bad?" she asked, looking up at him with worried eyes.

Ricardo laughed behind them, and Ian turned around. He'd almost forgotten they were surrounded by his coworkers on the set. When he was with Grace, the only thing that existed was Grace, it seemed.

"What's so funny?" Ian asked.

"You two are funny," Ricardo said, shaking his head. "It was a great scene. We're going to have tons of subscribers emailing us to see more of 'Honey'—you know that, right?"

Grace raised her eyebrows as if the thought hadn't occurred to her. It seemed she had no idea how incredible she was. How sexy.

"It's up to you," Ian said to her. Ever since he'd been with Grace, he felt less of need to work as a professional Dom. Not when he had Grace to play with. No other woman could submit to him in the bedroom with that same trusting, loving look in her eye. It made being with the actresses on the set seem like he was going through the motions.

"Maybe if I could wear one of those little half-masks, the kind with sequins? Something to hide my face but make me look interesting," Grace mused.

"Maybe Ricardo could find another Dom and you and I could just shoot our own scenes for the site," Ian suggested, speaking the idea before the full implication of his words hit him.

"What?" Ricardo's face went from amused to pissed-off in a fraction of a second. "Find another Dom? And what are you gonna do for a job?"

Ian shrugged. "If Grace wants to, we can still shoot scenes for you together. But I'm feeling ready to move on to something else."

Hell, maybe he could even go back to law, as long as he had Grace to come home to at night. With her, it seemed like he really could have it all.

Grace looked up at him surprise. "I'd be happy to do videos with you for the website, and I hate to admit that I love the idea of you not shooting with other girls anymore...but I don't want to be the one who pulls you out of your lifestyle."

Ian smiled. He had no intention of leaving the lifestyle. He was never truly in it. His kinks, his desires, Grace could fulfill them all. With her, he could have the one thing he never thought possible: a typical life with a kinky nightlife. He didn't need to be Master all day long. If Grace were his wife, they'd be equals, partners.

Until bedtime. They'd make up their own sort of BDSM lifestyle as went. Those "one true way-ers" on the forums annoyed the hell out of him anyway. He didn't care about making random strangers feel justified. As long as Grace was happy, as long as she'd be his—

Wait a minute, wife?

Since when did he look at a woman and think about her likelihood as a good wife? Since Grace. Since now.

"What do you say, Grace? We could make a great team. Lawyer and nurse by day, Master and slave by night."

"We already do make a great team," she looked back over at the spanking bench with a sexy smile. "And we both like late-night pancakes, which pretty much means we're soulmates. I think I learned that in nursing school."

"Is that a yes?" he asked, needing to know they were on the same page. "Official girlfriend, official but occasional sex-slave?"

"Wow, you really are a lawyer, aren't you," she teased. "Yes, officially, yes."

Ian picked her up and kissed her hard. "Consider this my notice, Ricardo. We'll be back to shoot some more scenes tomorrow night. And in the meantime, you might want to start auditioning Doms."

"So I'm a porn star now," Grace said breathlessly. "Does this mean I'm not a nice, respectable girl anymore?"

"You did exactly what you wanted to do, and I absolutely respect you for it," he replied. Unshed tears glittered in her eyes. "Wait, why are you crying? I was being serious."

"I know you were."

And she kissed him back.

The End

ABOUT SHOSHANNA EVERS

New York Times and USA Today Bestselling author Shoshanna Evers has written dozens of sexy stories, including The Man Who Holds the Whip (part of the bestselling MAKE ME anthology), Overheated, The Enslaved Trilogy, and The Pulse Trilogy (from Simon & Schuster Pocket Star).

Her work has been featured in Best Bondage Erotica 2012 and Best Bondage Erotica 2013, the Penguin/Berkley Heat anthology Agony/Ecstasy, and numerous erotic BDSM novellas including Chastity Belt and Punishing the Art Thief from Ellora's Cave Publishing.

Her two bestselling non-fiction writing anthologies include How To Write Hot Sex: Tips from Multi-Published Erotic Romance Authors, and Successful Self-Publishing: How We Do It (And How You Can Too).

Shoshanna is also the cofounder of SelfPubBookCovers.com, the largest selection of instantly customizable, one-of-a-kind, premade book covers in the world.

Shoshanna Evers has been listed on Amazon as one of the "Most Popular Authors in Romance," as well as on the Contemporary Romance, and Erotica "Most Popular

Authors" lists.

Reviewers have called Shoshanna's writing "fast paced, intense, and sexual…every naughty fantasy come to life for the reader" with stories where "the plot is fresh and the pacing excellent, the emotions…real and poignant."

Shoshanna used to work as a syndicated advice columnist and a registered nurse, but now she's a full-time smut writer and a home-schooling mom. She lives with her family and two big dogs in Northern Idaho.

Shoshanna Evers wants you to stay in touch!
Like erotic romance? Sign up for Shoshanna Evers's newsletter (ShoshannaEvers.com/blog) *to be notified when a new book releases (right side of the page!)*

Visit ShoshannaEvers.com for monthly giveaways
and red-hot excerpts!
Let's be BFF's!

Website: ShoshannaEvers.com
Newsletter (right side of the page!): ShoshannaEvers.com/blog
Blog: TheWritersChallenge.com
Twitter: Twitter.com/ShoshannaEvers
Facebook: Facebook.com/shoshanna.evers
Goodreads: goodreads.com/shoshannaevers
Email: shoshanna.evers@gmail.com

Shoshanna's book cover website (thousands and thousands of one-of-a-kind premade covers you can instantly customize): **SelfPubBookCovers.com**

ACKNOWLEDGEMENTS

Thank you to my cover designer Rob Sturtz at SelfPubBookCovers.com for creating a one-of-a-kind cover, to erotic romance author Cara Bristol and my first agent, Courtney Miller-Callihan, for beta-reading this book, and to my assistant Annette Stone of Authors Assistance Agency, you are a huge help!

Thank you to Skye Warren for including *The Man Who Holds the Whip* in the *New York Times* and *USA Today* bestselling box set, MAKE ME: Twelve Tales of Dark Desire.

And thank you to my readers. You are the reason I write, I love you all. If you enjoyed this book, it would be wonderful if you could leave a review on the site where you purchased it. I look forward to hearing what you think!

Please stay in touch and connect with me...

on Twitter @ShoshannaEvers,

Facebook at www.facebook.com/shoshanna.evers

and via my newsletter (sign up on my website www.ShoshannaEvers.com if you haven't already!)

www.ingramcontent.com/pod-product-compliance
Lightning Source LLC
Chambersburg PA
CBHW030555130626
46552CB00006B/2562